THE GO-BACKER

Peter R. Decker '57

BY PETER R. DECKER

Western Slope Press

This is a work of fiction. Names, characters, organizations, places, events, and incidents are either products of the author's imagination or are used fictitiously.

Copyright © 2017 Peter R. Decker

All rights reserved.

No part of this book may be reproduced, or stored in a retrieval system, or transmitted in any form or by any means, electronic, mechanical, photocopying, recording, or otherwise, without express written permission of the publisher.

Published by Western Slope Press

 Edited and Designed by Girl Friday Productions
www.girlfridayproductions.com

Editorial: Lindsey Alexander, Monique Vescia
Interior Design: Rachel Marek
Cover Design: William Matthews
Image Credits: painting by William Matthews

ISBN (Paperback): 9780999369203
e-ISBN: 9780999369210

First Edition

Printed in the United States of America

AUTHOR'S NOTE

One iconic image in American history is that of a covered wagon train crossing the central plains. The white canvas caravan portrays in part the story of our western settlement fostered by the Homestead Act of 1862 ("an Act to Secure Homesteads to Actual Settlers on the Public Domain"). The homesteader represents the embodiment of Thomas Jefferson's idealized "yeoman farmer."

Thousands of personal diaries and letters provide further evidence of this romanticized adventure. The theme in these personal writings is usually the same: we hearty homesteaders succeeded in making a new home for ourselves by our toughness and perseverance. This is all true, of course. But what's missing are the stories of those who started out with the intention to homestead but who, in the end, never succeeded in attaining their dream. They gave up the effort for a variety of reasons. Pioneers[1] who stayed the course referred to them as "the go-backers." We now know that seven out of ten homestead seekers failed to attain their dream. The failure rate is

---

1 The word *pioneer* is derived from the French term for "foot soldier."

higher when those homesteaders who "proved up" but soon thereafter "starved out." They either went home or made a new beginning usually east of the West's high plains.

Hardly any attention has been given to these go-backers, especially by historians. Academics are confronted with a multitude of diaries and letters that portray the homesteading experience as something akin to Laura Ingalls Wilder's *Little House on the Prairie*, with very little attention to why some pioneers failed to attain their dream. No one likes to write about their own failures.

Maybe that is why Hamlin Garland, in his book *Main-Travelled Roads*, wanted to remind us that frontier life was too often romanticized: "Milking as depicted on a blue china plate where a maid in a flounced petticoat is caressing a gentle cow in a field of daisies is quite unlike sitting down to the steaming flank of a stinking brindle heifer in fly time."

Yes, frontier life was a tough gamble. It was not for the weak of heart, the pessimist, or the destitute. The weak succumbed to disease and death; accidents were common, and misinformation even more common. The lives and accomplishments of the pioneers who stayed the course deserve our admiration. The go-backers, and their experiences, deserve our attention as well.

April 1865, Northern Virginia

In the mid-morning humidity, the Tenth Vermont Infantry stood in formation before a rail siding, waiting impatiently to board the vacant cattle cars, the only roiling stock available at the end of the war, that would return them home to Vermont by way of Washington, Baltimore, New York, and Albany. First Sergeant Calvin Marlow ordered his weary company to gather up their knapsacks and climb into the two cattle cars designated for his C Company, their home for the next five days. The regimental officers had already made themselves comfortable in their parlor car at the rear of the ten-car train. The non-walking wounded, attended to by three male nurses, found some relief in the single hospital car behind the officers' car. The mess car rode directly in front of the eight troop cars, where it served up its excuse for food and tepid water from the sliding doorway when it stopped at 1200 hours and 1800 hours. The soldiers arranged themselves as best they could in the packed cars. They stood or lay down on the manure-covered floors. The wooden-slatted cattle cars did provide them shade from the blazing Virginia sun but not relief from the humidity, which only heightened the manure's ammonia stench, an added irritant to the soldiers' lungs and eyes.

Once inside the car, Calvin shouted above the noise of the grumbling soldiers. "You troops in that far corner, listen up. Bust through the floorboards and make me a crap hole . . . a big one, and I mean real fast."

A strong voice returned the command: "Will do, Chief." The platoon sergeants frequently used the moniker when addressing Calvin, with his high cheekbones and bronze-colored skin of an Indian.

The smell of human vomit soon added to that of animal feces. *Could this be our final fate,* Calvin asked himself, *squeezed into these coffin cars, with little water or food, left to rot after our service to the Union? For all of our Christian efforts, is this our gift from God?*

The soldiers around Calvin eased back into the car to give their company sergeant space to lay his short, stocky body on the floor after he'd relieved his bowels. His back and thickly muscled shoulders ached from the long march earlier in the day. He walked with the physique and posture of a forward-leaning plowman. Indeed, plowing was a task he knew all too well, with his burly arms stiff by his sides as if holding two plow handles. His gray-blue eyes always focused to the front, and he remained unaware of the sweat dripping from his short sandy hair, down his cheeks, and through the thick whiskers covering his prominent chin.

Calvin had ridden a train only once before when, three years earlier, he had volunteered to join Vermont's newest regiment of eight hundred soldiers and officers, which assembled in Rutland in the spring of 1862. Like Calvin, the volunteers were mostly farmers or tradesmen, except for the lone Negro volunteer, an assistant to a blacksmith, who was turned away.

Now, three years later, the regiment numbered only 550 soldiers. Left behind were 104 dead from combat or disease, another 89 seriously wounded, two suicides, and the rest unaccounted for—assumed to have been taken prisoner or deserted.

Waiting in the steaming heat for what seemed like two hours, the soldiers asked themselves, *Is this the way the army rewards us after we fought like hell for the Union? It deposits us in cattle cars lined with shit and feeds us food loaded with mold? Surely the Rebel prisoners are treated better. Just get this train moving and get us the hell out of here and home to see our families.*

Yes, Calvin thought, *back to my farm to see my children and forget the war forever.*

But Calvin found it difficult to forget the war when his memory wouldn't release it. He could remember all too well the death of his company comrades, especially his bunkmate Patrick Keating, from Rutland. Two years earlier, at the Battle of Chancellorsville, Patrick had rushed with Calvin from their trench when their company charged across an open meadow under heavy Rebel fire from the woods beyond. Calvin remembered the explosion. Mortar fragments cut into his right cheek and knee as the blast knocked him to the ground. He rolled over and grabbed his bleeding knee, now exposed from beneath his blue trousers. There, off to his right, lay Patrick on his back, his eyes open and looking upward from his jawless head. Four other Vermonters lay dead, twisted in grotesque shapes, with blood leaking from their gruesome open wounds. Others lay screaming for help and pleading for comrades to put them down like injured horses. Calvin was immobilized by fear, his hands shaking, unable to reload his Springfield.

When the infantry company moved forward, finally reaching the shelter of trees, the Rebels retreated from the overwhelming artillery support given the Vermonters. The weeklong battle at Chancellorsville ended in a Rebel victory, but at great cost to both sides. That evening, Calvin, like other company sergeants, ordered his troops to recover the wounded and dead. With the help of a lantern, the sergeant limped and stumbled over bodies, searching for Keating. He found him lying in a pool of black blood, his gray eyes still open and staring upward. He dragged him by his only attached arm across a battlefield littered with dead or moaning soldiers and into the trees, where he placed Keating in the assembled row of corpses, their blood now caked black on their open wounds and tattered blue uniforms. Calvin withdrew a diary and small wallet from Patrick's knapsack before another soldier covered him with a canvas sheet. Orderlies searched the line of stiff, bloated bodies for personal items, bagged them, and tied the bags to the toes or fingers of the dead. A medical corpsman bandaged Calvin's wounds and told him how lucky he was that his wounds had not become infected. "You can see what happens to an infected leg or arm," the corpsman said as he pointed to a pile of human limbs stacked outside the surgeon's tent.

"You need to stay off your leg for a couple of days," the corpsman continued as he gently guided Calvin to the ground, "then you can go be a hero."

"I have no urge to be a hero," Calvin replied. "Heroes are made where the fighting is the fiercest. If I end up a dead hero, I don't get paid any more than the worst laggard. Besides, it takes courage to be a hero, a quality I seem not to have acquired. Be assured, however, I'll fight on, not to be a hero, but to stay alive and see my family."

April 1865, Northern Virginia

The train finally started to move. "Faster, faster!" soldiers shouted, knowing the train was capable of a quicker pace. Instead of moving at the rate of a galloping horse as they hoped, it crawled like an injured turtle. The soldiers occupied their time in the cattle cars recounting battles and listing dead friends, talking about their families at home, and picking lice off one another's filthy bodies. They crept along at maybe five miles an hour until they cleared Washington and made their way to Baltimore. Suddenly, the train stopped and backed into a siding where a clean-shaven officer shouted for attention from each car. "President Lincoln was shot last evening and died early this morning. We expect to receive further orders within the hour." The soldiers sat or lay stunned by the news. Many openly wept, including some who hated what they thought to be Lincoln's wasteful war to end slavery.

    The officer again made an announcement two hours later. "We are to proceed on to Baltimore to await further orders. In Baltimore, you will leave your present quarters and be free to visit the city." A great cheer went up from the soldiers. "But you will be back at your railcar in company formation by 0600 tomorrow. If you are absent or late, you will be subject to severe punishment. Understood?" Then the officer looked at Calvin. "Company sergeants will take the roll in the morning."

A rumor quickly spread through the ranks that the regiment would return to the Army of the Potomac. The rumor put a damper on the enthusiasm generated by the news of a short twelve-hour leave. Once the train arrived in Baltimore, the soldiers made a quick exit from the railcars after the discomfort of having been crammed into their filthy interiors for over twelve hours.

Once free to roam Baltimore, regimental discipline quickly dissolved into disorderly conduct, including brawls between the soldiers and civilian sympathizers of the Confederate cause. A distinct Southern accent signaled an immediate enemy. Saloons that refused to serve rowdy soldiers were in some cases torched. The soldiers felt that those "nigger city workers" had not shown proper respect for their military service and sacrifice. Fights broke out between the battle-hardened veterans and a celebratory mob of self-described freemen. The next day the Baltimore police announced the murder of five residents: four Negro workers and a white Southerner whose verbal defense of the Confederacy had no doubt offended a Green Mountain soldier. Baltimore authorities called a meeting with the regiment's senior officers to announce they wanted the Vermonters collected up and moved out of town, by foot or by train, but "make it fast."

Calvin's company staggered into formation before 0600 the next morning. The platoon sergeants reported eight missing soldiers from the company, including one dead, three in the city hospital, and four others presumably passed out in some Baltimore alley. Once again, Calvin ordered the company into their respective cars and barked out to them, "Put the rabbit in your foot and get yourselves into those cars. Those of you too drunk to move, retch outside the car, not in it." He said in an aside to one of the platoon sergeants, "This war sure as hell stirred up animosity between whites and Negroes."

The train finally crept into Brattleboro on May 10, after constant delays caused by higher-priority freight trains.

The soldiers, who prided themselves on being the "Green Mountain Boys," exhibited a sense of entitlement as they sought out food, liquor, and a bath. Three vendors handed out fresh beef and vegetables to honor the Vermont veterans; one bar offered free beer until it ran out. After a few drinks, soldiers rushed to the Connecticut River, stripped off their lice-infested uniforms, and jumped into the icy-cold water.

August 1869; Brattleboro, Vermont

Not until mid-August did the army allow the Vermont regiment to disband from its temporary camp in Brattleboro. To relieve the boredom, company commanders invented an array of useless duties for their troops to perform. Calvin, as company sergeant, ordered one platoon to chop enough wood to supply the entire army with warmth for a whole year. He detailed another platoon the daily chore of polishing the brass plates on their five cannons and cleaning the more than five hundred Springfields, none of which had been fired in over four months. The third platoon was made to replace all tent ropes, needed or not. The company troops complained but knew full well that the company commander, not First Sergeant Calvin Marlow, had devised their silly tasks.

At the final regimental formation, the colonel read off the names of the regiment's dead, thanked the survivors for their service, and expressed his pride in the regiment's battle victories. Finally, he ended his remarks with, "You Green Mountain Boys are now free to go home. Dismissed." A cheer went up, loud enough to be heard in Washington.

Calvin connected with three other comrades who farmed near him in Shoreham alongside Lake Champlain, halfway up the Vermont side to Canada. The three soldiers had hoped to make at least fifteen miles a day with their packs, but when reminded of Calvin's knee, they planned on slower progress. Each volunteered to carry Calvin's knapsack to lighten his load and, hopefully, quicken the pace. The soldiers unbuttoned their woolen tunics to cool themselves in the brisk late-summer breeze. Calvin worked himself into the steady step of a plowman, a pace he had perfected over twenty years as a farmer in Connecticut and later in Vermont.

Silently, the four soldiers plodded north, their eyes on the hilly road, with only side glances at the passing farms. Families offered them mint tea, and often a meal and a night's protection in a barn from the evening chill or a rain shower. The older farmers, too old for the war, questioned them constantly. What can you tell us about the new president? We read the South will not make peace with him. Why? Will those freed Negroes be moving north? What about them Rebels? Did we kick their asses hard enough so they won't want to fight again? Ever get to meet General Grant or Sherman? I hear Sherman is one ornery son of a bitch. Is that true? After an evening's rest, the soldiers stashed leftovers from their free supper in their knapsacks and filled their canteens with sugared cold tea.

Along the roads, the soldiers were stunned to see so many untended fields. Dead cornstalks, normally as high as the top of a scarecrow, stood limp, awaiting some moisture. Corncribs appeared mostly empty, the sign of a poor summer crop. Fewer dairy cows and sheep grazed the dun pastures, and the workhorses looked to be short on groceries. The milk barns needed repair, and too many rocks and weeds lay scattered on the dry hay fields.

In Rutland, on an overcast day, Calvin parted company with his three fellow travelers—all headed north to Colchester and Burlington—and sought out Patrick Keating's farm. With directions from a local blacksmith, he located it—a small place with sheep six miles west of town. In the fenced yard, a dog rushed at him, barking angrily, before a young woman on the front porch yelled at the mutt. Calvin approached her slowly, not knowing what to say. To identify himself from a distance and outside the fence, he shouted his name, "the army bunkmate of Patrick." She ran to Calvin, threw her arms around him, and said through her tears, "I know you, Calvin, from Patrick's letters. He was so fond of you, said you were his best friend. The army informed me by letter of his death only a month or so ago. Did he die without pain, I pray?"

"Yes," Calvin lied softly.

The two of them sat on the porch looking west toward an apple orchard and, in the distance, the gray waters of Lake Champlain. They talked about Patrick, his pleasure in serving with Vermont's Green Mountain Boys, like his grandfather before him, and the pride Patrick expressed in his letters for the regiment's victories.

"Yes," Calvin responded, "and he did so with bravery and few complaints . . . except maybe for the food and the slow mail. He saved all your letters. I have them here in this small package, along with his diary and a few other personal items. I thought you'd want them." She took the canvas-covered package as if accepting a Bible, kissed it, and wept.

Once composed, she continued, "I couldn't afford to have him brought back home and buried here. The army assured me he will be buried properly in a military cemetery with other Union soldiers in Virginia . . . separate from the Rebels, I hope."

Calvin bid Mrs. Keating a hasty good-bye before she could ask for more details about the war and the circumstances of Patrick's violent death.

After his detour to the Keating farm, he made up time with an occasional lift in a farm wagon driven by a family happy to aid a limping veteran. More questions, of course. What do you know about Andrew Johnson, the new president? Will the South rise again as suggested in the *Rutland Herald*?

September 1865; Shoreham, Vermont

Finally, after a week's hike from Brattleboro, Calvin arrived at the rutted lane leading up to his small white farmhouse. He leaned over and kissed the ground, then took a generous lick of the soil. He limped past the small cornfield close to the farmhouse and noticed immediately the dead leaves hanging from the stunted cornstalks. The woodpile had shrunk to less than a half cord. He noticed also that most of the paint on the barn's north side had peeled off to reveal the weathered gray boards underneath. Roof shingles were missing, as were chunks of mortar from the barn's foundation. He whistled toward the barn and, as he hoped, Dan—the oldest of the three Morgan workhorses—whinnied as he stuck his head out the top of the Dutch door, his ears perked forward atop his coal-black head.

As Calvin approached the front porch and limped up the broken steps, he could hear the children's laughter. He dropped his pack and swung open the front door. The children—Hiram, age twelve; his younger brother, Sam, age nine; and their sister, Cornelia, age seven—glanced up from the floor at their unrecognizable father, a hollow-eyed stranger. He filled the room with the bitter smell of sweat as the children stared in fear at the dark-bearded intruder. They said nothing, transfixed as if frozen in the presence of a ghost. As he said their names, his faint voice sounded like that of an imagined phantom from inside the thicket of his beard. Then, in a stronger voice, he called out, "Grace, where are you?!" She rushed in from the kitchen toward the familiar sound, threw her arms around Calvin's shoulders, and together they cried uncontrollably.

At supper that evening, Calvin answered questions about the never-ending marches and battles, and how the Vermonters helped win a decisive victory—but without the details of war.

He described the destruction of two Southern cities and the defense of a Northern city—New York, two years before, when his company was pulled out of Virginia and sent by train to the city to help put down the unruly mobs during their draft riots. "The city's Irish workers wanted no part of a war to free Negroes, who would replace them in the city's workforce after the war," Calvin explained. "And not a one of them Irishmen had three hundred dollars to buy a substitute for themselves in the event they were drafted." Calvin's voice softened as he continued, "The rioters sacked shops, saloons, and the homes of antislavery leaders and killed hundreds of Negroes. Finally, the undermanned city police, with the army's assistance, put an end to the riots. From what I saw, the Negroes in the South were a lot better off than they were in the North. It wasn't what I expected."

After the young ones were put to bed, Calvin and Grace talked about the children and the farm late into the evening. Without asking too many questions, Calvin said he could see that the thirty-acre farm had produced a poor crop. Grace quickly defended Hiram and the neighbor's young boy she had hired to help with the farmwork and blamed the poor crop on the hot, dry summer.

Grace further explained, "I loaded some of the corncribs last fall after the boys helped with the shucking. I managed to sell fifteen bushels at the Middlebury market for not much cash. I fed some corn to the three ewes after they'd eaten their pasture to the bare roots. Then, two days later, the three of them suddenly bloated and died. The veterinarian in Middlebury said their intestines had exploded because of the corn. For two months, we bottle-fed the bum lambs and then sold them for need of cash." Grace's eyes watered again when she informed Calvin, for the first time, about her mother's sudden death in Connecticut.

She turned to Calvin, wiped her eyes, and continued, "She died of a heart attack in the summer's heat. If not for the help of a large bank draft from my brother, Jonathan, after he sold Mother's farm, the children and I would have starved to death last winter. It's been a hard year, Calvin." He noticed the new stress lines on her forehead, others around her fatigued eyes, and deeper marks etched at each side of her mouth. Her callused hands and ragged clothing added to the image of an exhausted woman. He had also seen the dark circles beneath their once-bright eyes, now burned out; their threadbare clothing hung loosely on their bony frames. Young Hiram's boots had worn-through soles, and only dirty newspapers guarded his callused feet from the ground beneath.

Grace, wiping her eyes, continued, "I don't know if I can take another winter like last year, Calvin." He reached over, held her wet face between his rough hands, and kissed her. He could not remember her so depressed, not even after she'd lost their first baby at birth. She always looked at life with patience, hope, and courage—a bigger crop with higher prices, a quick and full recovery from an injury or disease—sometimes, yes, with a feeling of sadness, but not for long. Self-pity had never found a place in her heart. She sparkled like an evening star at a child's new skill or the birth of a lamb. Her natural beauty and tenderness always lit up Calvin's days after long hours in the field.

The next day, shadowed by Hiram and Sam, Calvin completed an inspection of the farm. He checked the condition of the milk cow and the Morgan horses, took an inventory of available food for the family and winter feed for the livestock, inspected the condition of the farm's three buildings, and compiled an estimate for needed repairs. He recognized immediately that it would take all winter and then some to put the farm back into a semblance of working order. Thankfully, the Morgan team had remained in good flesh and their harness had been well cared for. The farm wagon, however, the most critical piece of equipment for personal and farm transportation, needed a complete overhaul. Together with Grace, he reviewed all that needed to be accomplished on the farm before next spring. Grace volunteered, "There are going to be some expensive repairs, especially the barn and the wagon." Calvin nodded in agreement.

The next day, market Friday, Calvin loaded the family into the wagon and set off for Middlebury, the county seat and its largest town. On the way, he talked to the Morgan team, Dan and Butch, to accustom them once again to his voice and familiarize them with his commands. They never missed a beat. He remarked to Grace how in his absence so little had changed along the road; only a half-built barn caught his attention. The fields appeared untended, with too many rocks and weeds choking the wilted cornstalks. Maybe the stone walls appeared a bit higher, but they needed repair. In town, the family stared in the shop windows at the ready-made clothes, which they very much needed but could ill afford. With some of the proceeds from Grace's bank draft, the Marlows did buy some fresh fruit, three pounds of boned beef, and new leather boots for the children before heading to the town's wagon shop, owned by Lester Worley.

"What will it take to fix this broken-down crate?" Calvin asked Lester.

"Welcome home, Calvin. Good to see you looking so healthy," Lester replied, something of an exaggeration given that Calvin had shed close to twenty pounds in Virginia and on the road. "Sure needs some work, it does," the wagon maker said, looking at the wagon. "Them wheels are shot, and look at dem spokes—some are rotten to the core. The running gear is about to break apart, and the tongue needs to be replaced. By the time you add up all those replacements and my labor, hell, you'd be better off buyin' a new one." Calvin somehow knew that answer before Lester offered it.

"That one over there . . . it's a humdinger," Lester continued as he pointed to one of five wagons lined up outside his shop. "I sold one just like it last week to a farmer, Sam Case, down south in Brandon. You know him? Said he's a movin' west because he's tired of farmin' rocks and milkin' dry cows twice a day. 'No sirree, not for me,' he said. He wanted somethin' real stout to get him to the goldfields. I sold him the four-by-twelve-foot model for eighty in gold, along with that guidebook about travelin' west. Good solid white oak, it is. Notice that the two rear-wheel brakes are controlled by just one handle. My own invention, it is. And that there guidebook is real interestin'. Sold six of 'em just in the last month. An army man wrote it. He's been all over the West; knows the country like the palm of his hand, or so he says. The book tells you what to take if you're headed out west to homestead or to dig for gold and how to get there."

Calvin walked over and inspected the new wagon. Just as Lester said, it was well built of sturdy white oak with strong birch hoops to support a canvas bonnet. The tongue was stout too. He picked up a copy of *Prairie Traveler*, written by Captain Randolph Marcy. *Must be OK if it's published by the War Department*, he thought.

"I'll buy the book, but not the wagon. Haven't the cash right now to buy a new one or repair the old one."

"The book is on me. It's good reading. You take care, Calvin, and it sure is good to have you back here."

On the way home, Calvin made a stop at the candy store before crossing the wooden bridge over Middlebury's Otter Creek. "Lester talks about a replacement for our wagon. What he needs to do first is get this damned town to replace the wooden planks on this dilapidated bridge. Most of 'em are rotten. Horse could break a leg if a driver's not careful," he shouted to Grace over the noise of the nearby waterfall.

That evening at home, Grace and Calvin sat talking before a fire, once again about the farm, the children, and the family's future prospects.

Grace looked up from her knitting and said in a serious tone, "When you were gone, I read some articles in the *New England Farmer* about new farming opportunities in the Old Northwest Territory and some of the lands west of the Mississippi now open for settlement with President Lincoln's Homestead Act. You remember the Sheltons just up the road from us? They left early in April for the West, and I've heard at the market how others around here are preparing to do the same. As Mr. Worley said, not much profit in farmin' rocks, especially with corn prices being what they are. Since you've been away, Calvin, corn around here won't put clothes on the children or food on the table. *New England Farmer* says it's the Erie Canal over in New York that's killing us, bringing all that western grain into eastern markets and depressing our prices. Those western corn growers are making bushels of money at our expense . . . maybe that's another reason to think about moving from here."

Calvin listened in surprise to Grace's suggestion about moving. He remembered the one time before the war that they'd had a brief conversation about moving. "Absolutely not," said Grace in a firm manner. "We have our church here and good neighbors." End of conversation. *Now she's thinking about a move. She's had a hard time here alone during the war. I can't blame her,* Calvin thought.

He picked up on her idea of moving, and in an attempt to keep the conversation alive, he said, "Remember just before the war, folks were attracted west by the discovery of gold in California and Colorado? But now, as you suggest, the promise of free land with the new Homestead Act is attracting folks west. I think our regiment lost more deserters to the prospect of free land than we did to the gold mines. Some of my soldier buddies received letters from a few of these deserters who had settled out west. They wrote about the good farmland they'd seen. As I understand it, folks can move onto a homestead of 160 acres, and after five years of living on it and making some minimal improvements, the land is theirs with the payment of a small filing fee. But in our case, we'd only need three years on the homestead before we get title to the land because I understand that, as a veteran, I may get credit for my three years of service."

Calvin convinced Grace that they had few ties in Shoreham. "A few friends, yes, but with the Reverend Howland gone to Ohio, our connection to the Congregational church is almost severed. It's not as if we're going into a self-imposed exile. Here in the East, we have almost no family ties. My family is gone; so too is yours, except for your brother and two nephews. With that bank draft from the sale of your mother's farm, plus the sale of our farm and the payoff of our bank loan, we'd have cash enough to move ourselves west to a homestead."

"Maybe so, but where?"

"The railroad brochures I've read say most of the available land is on the far side of the Missouri River, like in Kansas, the Nebraska Territory, or the Colorado Territory. They mention all the rich farmland suitable for grains and good grass for livestock. They say it's safe now that the war has ended and the army has sent more troops to guard the new rail lines and homesteads."

Grace wanted some clarification from her husband. She asked, "The war with the Rebels may have ended, but what about those wild redskins out west? I hear stories about how they capture white people, torture them, and violate the women."

Calvin cautioned her not to take stock in such stories and assured her that recently the army had built new posts out west to keep the Indians on their own land and away from white settlers. "We could be one of the first families to settle on the fertile Indian ground that is now available with the Indians removed to reservations. Also, I understand the trails to those lands are well marked and protected by army troops. Can't be too dangerous if the Sheltons moved west like you said. Hell, Old Man Shelton's got to be well into his sixties, and he's always feared his own shadow."

"Not a word from them since they left," Grace observed.

Calvin informed Grace about the slow mails from the West and then added, "Old Man Shelton couldn't write his own name to endorse a hundred-dollar check if his life depended on it. Besides, if it's so dangerous out west, with so few opportunities, why have so many folks already moved there? It is not like we'd be the first pioneers moving out there . . . more like followers."

Grace let Calvin know she had no intention of going west in search of gold. "Let others do that; for them it's all about money. That's not the life I know or want for us. I only want to live on some good farmland so we can do what we know best. I've had enough of plowing in these uneven, rocky fields, thick with clay. As you know, this is no country for growing corn, or any type of grain for that matter. We'd have been better off had we stayed in Connecticut years ago. For all our hard labor, Calvin, look at our meager earnings. I feel imprisoned here in this spring mud. Maybe we can do better for our children someplace else."

"You make it sound as if we have no choices for our future. Of course we do. You've always been so adventurous. What's changed with you? Think of our move as an adventure, a new beginning for the two of us and the children."

"It's my energy, Calvin," she said as her eyes filled. "Yes, I'd like to pick up and move, but at the same time, we have good friends and neighbors here who've looked after us when we needed them. I'm not certain the children or I can survive a long wagon trip to wherever it is you want to go."

Then Grace strengthened her voice and said, "I think you need to research our destination and how we can get there safely. Until you do, I have no plans of moving and living with a bunch of wild savages." Quick to respond, Calvin promised to inquire around town and go to the library to look through some magazines and newspapers.

At the Middlebury town library, Calvin read about the recently discovered and abundant natural resources available in the territories west of the Missouri River. And then, for some reason, he began to remember the war, the smell of death, battlefields littered with dead friends, and the barrage of constant orders: "Push 'em back and take this field." "Dig your foxholes deeper." "Tie a tourniquet between his elbow and shoulder." "Lead him back to the hospital tent." "Fire a volley into those bushes to the left of that big oak dead center ahead." "Take care of your feet, you only got one set, and they're your only transportation out of this hell."

I need to get away from Vermont, Calvin thought. *Maybe then I can rid my brain of these war memories. Oh, how I'd love to sleep through the night and not wake up the family with my screams. Maybe in the West I can cleanse my memory and body of the demons. I need a new life for myself with my family.*

At the Middlebury College library, Calvin found advertisements in a St. Louis paper for "superior agricultural land" offered by various railroad and land companies, but with few specifics about crops, soils, or climate. The paper also included reports from every major trailhead town along the Missouri River, from Council Bluffs, Iowa, to Westport, Kansas, and St. Joseph, Missouri, all proclaiming to those headed west the superiority of their respective markets. An Omaha paper advised: "Yes, it takes fortitude on the part of the hearty and enterprising pioneers to move west along the Oregon Trail, but they'll need the best supplies once they reach the rich farmlands west of the Missouri or the goldfields of Colorado." The agricultural correspondent for the *Missouri Republican* claimed he'd never seen any better grass country than in western Nebraska and eastern Colorado, where "the farming possibilities are endless." A *New York Tribune* editorial claimed that all citizens who wanted to advance the nation's prosperity "could help the cause by taking up residence in the new fertile lands of the West." The paper claimed that those who moved west and followed the mandate of Manifest Destiny were the "true postwar patriots." Calvin had to agree with Horace Greeley's editorials, which fed his patriotic instincts and his inclination to join the adventurous movement westward.

The idea of moving west, or "westering," as the newspapers called it, captured his imagination and monopolized all his thoughts. He knew he could put thousands of miles between his old life in Vermont and the memories he attached to the state to build a new life on a fertile homestead. Like so many other New Englanders, Calvin wanted to ride the tide to "the sunset region." There, he imagined a new and comfortable life for his children, far different from his harsh childhood living under the thumb of his father, who hurled tools at him from the workbench and tied him and his Indian friend, the hired hand, to a wagon wheel for two hours in the midday sun. He remembered the threat from his father: "Don't screw up again, or you'll spend all day on the wheel."

Calvin made the journey to the West sound like an exciting adventure for the children, and Grace agreed, except for his idea of taking a wagon ride as far as Oregon. Calvin researched other, closer destinations appropriate for farming. Colorado Territory kept appearing as a favored destination for gold-seeking miners and for farmers to feed them.

After further research, it became apparent to Calvin that he'd underestimated the cost of travel, especially the rail fares. He found the canal fees more reasonable, but the papers warned about the availability of canal boats and barges: "There are long wagon lines waiting to cross the rivers," they cautioned. He studied three different travel guides in addition to the *Prairie Traveler*. One guide confirmed the presence of Indians and occasional attacks, but every guidebook noted that such danger could be easily avoided by traveling in a wagon train under the direction of an experienced trail guide. Newspapers also reported that the army had recently built new camps and forts in the West to protect the telegraph lines, railroad crews, overland trails, and the new white settlements along the Platte River.

March 1866; Shoreham, Vermont

Grace and Calvin spent hours discussing the move and considering all the details. What trails and canals should they follow? Should they use horses to pull the wagon? What maps, food, clothing, and medicine should they bring, and how much? Would they need a lot of cash? What should they leave behind? Captain Randolph Marcy, the army explorer and experienced traveler who wrote *Prairie Traveler*, recommended oxen rather than horses or mules. "Oxen can pull more weight and, once trained for the trail, move about three miles an hour or more . . . and can, in an emergency, be used for beef." He also advised against traveling by way of canals when possible because of their expense.

At supper, Calvin read aloud to Grace from the guidebook: "Avoid an overloaded or heavy Conestoga wagon. The wheels will sink into the sandy soil on the trail. For hunting and in the event of hostile Indians, be sure to have with you a breech-loading rifle and a Colt revolver. Wool clothing is recommended for the sudden changes of temperature. Woolen socks and heavy boots are mandatory, as are blankets, quinine, opium, camphor, some cathartic medicine, and brandy for snake bites."

"We sure need to stock up on some brandy," Calvin volunteered with a grin. Grace returned his comment with a nasty frown.

In preparation for the trip, they made lists, adding and crossing off items, mostly bulky and heavy furniture, trying to limit their cargo to fifteen hundred pounds.

At the Middlebury town library, Calvin also learned that in Burlington, the state's largest city and the site of the army's only active post in Vermont, he could find detailed maps of the West. For two days he studied and made notes from the maps, especially those of the western end of the Erie Canal, searching for the most direct route to a jumping-off site to the land west of the Missouri River. An army officer at the Burlington post who had recently returned from Fort Kearny in Nebraska told him about numerous roads west through Ohio, Indiana, Illinois, and Iowa to the jumping-off towns of Council Bluffs, Westport, and St. Joseph. He recommended Council Bluffs on the Missouri. "There you'll find some experienced ex-army officers assembling wagon trains and serving as train captains. But by no means," he warned Calvin, "should you travel alone." Before leaving Burlington, Calvin managed to locate a relatively new army tent, which he purchased for ten dollars.

In town, Calvin sold the old farm wagon to Lester Worley for fifteen dollars, and with an additional sixty in cash he bought a new twelve-foot-by-four-foot, two-thousand-pound oak wagon. It had two-foot-high slanted sides, four-foot rear wheels, and three-foot front ones. Calvin hated to sell off part of the Morgan team, his pride and joy, but even with the money from the three lambs and the milk cow, he needed the cash. He looked at a pair of well-trained mules offered at seventy dollars but instead purchased a yoke of two oxen for fifty dollars, each with a nose ring and, according to the seller, semi-broke to reins. The proceeds from the sale of Grace's family farm also allowed the Marlows to purchase two new water barrels; three tin canisters for salt pork, cornmeal, flour, and dried apples; and three watertight rubber sacks for beans, salt, sugar, coffee, baking soda, and seed grains (wheat, oats, and corn). Calvin lucked out and found a superb spyglass and two used weapons (a Colt pistol and an army carbine) and ammunition for each. Finally, he paid off the farm loan. The banker, Mr. Swift, said Calvin was one of his best customers and he was sorry to lose him to the pull of a homestead. "You take care, Calvin, on your travels west."

The young boys, Hiram and his brother, Sam, cried for days after they learned that part of the Morgan team, including their two favorite horses, had been sold along with the milk cow. Nothing would console them; they said they were not moving unless the horses accompanied them. But when Calvin told them that Barney, the Morgan stud, would come with them and that both of the boys would get to ride him on the trail west, their stubbornness dissolved.

The Stanahans, the Marlows' neighbors to the south, offered Calvin $380 for the farm, including some farm equipment that was too bulky to haul west. He pocketed $200 in specie and took a note for the remainder while making it absolutely clear that the final payment next year of $195 (including interest) needed to be paid in specie, not rag money.

The Marlows planned to take off after the mud season so as to be at the Erie Canal by the end of April. Grace, the family's weather forecaster, observed, "This year the March mud won't be out of here until May."

They made their preparations. Hiram oiled his new boots, Calvin sharpened everything with a blade on it, and Grace mended blankets and clothing. Occasionally, arguments broke out about what to take and what to leave or discard. Calvin won the argument to leave behind an oak armoire that they had hauled to Vermont from Grace's mother's house in Connecticut. The absence of the bulky family heirloom allowed more space for food barrels and canisters, a chest of clothes, miscellaneous tools, the sixty-pound John Deere plow, a spinning wheel, a mattress, two coal oil lanterns, and various cooking necessities—pot, frying pan, kettle, and small cookstove. Grace won the argument to take the Dutch oven and the heavy gilt-framed portrait of her father.

One evening Calvin wrote to Grace's brother.

Spring, 1866
Dear Jonathan,

I wanted to write you a personal note and thank you for all you have done to dispose of your family's farm and send Grace half the proceeds. That money has allowed us to pack up and leave Vermont for a new and hopefully better life in the West. We hear good things about eastern Colorado, where we hope to settle and farm.

Being a farmer yourself, you can understand that our farming life in Vermont has not been easy. In fact, making a living as a farmer is not easy even in the best of circumstances. We farmers are so dependent on the good graces of God, especially when it comes to weather. The drought last summer, for example, wreaked havoc with our crop. Then there is always sickness or an accident in the family, placing an additional burden on the healthy. I have never known a year when a family member hasn't come down with some ailment or had a bad accident. There never seems to be enough time in the day to accomplish what needs to be done, and then there is the added responsibly of being available to your neighbors when they need assistance for one thing or another. I remember one summer just before the war when Grace spent half her time helping a neighbor care for her aged father.

You've heard me say before that our Vermont farm grew more rocks than grain. Yes, the rocks made good walls or building foundations, but they didn't put food on the table or clothes on the children. Corn prices went to hell when the Erie Canal opened, and our church went in the same direction when our good reverend took another position in Ohio.

So off to the West we go, and with God's grace, we expect to make a new and better life. We will write along the way to keep you informed of our adventure.

With many thanks and appreciation to you, and with love to all,
Calvin

As Grace had predicted, the spring mud was slow to clear in Vermont. Nevertheless, the Marlows started off down the road on the eastern shore of Lake Champlain, its water still iced over, in late April. Another family had planned to join them on the trip to the Erie Canal but at the last minute dropped out because of the expense and danger.

While Calvin drove the wagon from the jockey box, Hiram rode Barney, and Grace, Sam, and Cornelia traveled in relative comfort in the wagon bed. After a day and a half on the road, they reached the southern end of the lake and Calvin located the entrance to the Champlain Canal, which would take them to the Hudson River. The canal's manager informed the Marlows they'd have to wait at least three days for some ice to clear before a barge could make it south to the Hudson River and the entrance to the Erie Canal. Impatient to keep moving and displeased with the high cost of the barge, Calvin decided to bypass the canal and proceed south by wagon along a road that ran parallel to the canal. Besides, he needed more time to perfect the skills necessary for driving a young, inexperienced oxen team. Already he missed his Morgan team, which was faster, more surefooted, and sure as hell smarter than the lumbering oxen.

Before heading to the Hudson, the family spent a layover day to rest the tired oxen. Calvin had the boys unhitch the wagon and search for patches of green grass for the livestock. Grace meanwhile repaired a small tear in the wagon's canvas bonnet and washed some clothes. Calvin plugged a leak in a water barrel and made some small adjustments to the wagon's running gear.

It took almost five days for the wagon to cover the sixty miles on the Champlain Canal road. The bulky oxen moved slowly on the muddy trail until they learned that Calvin's whip meant a faster pace. The family lost two days when they were delayed by an accident. The frozen ruts in the single-lane road didn't soften until well after noon. On one such icy hump, the wagon's contents shifted and a heavy crate smashed through a floor plank. It took an entire day to locate a lumber mill and a new plank, and a full morning the next day to rearrange barrels, boxes, and crates, then secure them again with ropes and thick rawhide strips. To make the wagon bed watertight, Calvin resealed the floorboard seams with strips of old rags soaked in bacon fat and then covered the seams with a new tar coating.

Early May 1866, Erie Canal to Toledo

Once they reached the Hudson, the family proceeded without incident to the Erie Canal entrance and the manager's office in Albany only to be told they'd have to wait at least two days for an available westbound barge to Buffalo. Once again, Calvin balked at the outrageous fare, twenty-four dollars for the wagon, livestock, and family.

The manager refused to negotiate and added, "Of course, you could swim it at no charge."

"But only if you swim and lead the way," Calvin spit back at him in a nasty tone of voice.

He noticed the listed fares posted on a handbill tacked to the wall. For an individual, the fare was six dollars, and for children under twelve, three dollars. Calvin came up with a cost-saving plan whereby Grace would take Cornelia with her on the barge while the boys and Calvin would take Barney, the wagon, and the oxen team on the canal path. He figured she'd probably be in Buffalo a day or so before the wagon. Besides, Sarah and Cornelia would be more comfortable on the ten-day, 363-mile trip. When Calvin made the arrangements with the manager and told him that he and his boys would be taking the wagon on the adjoining canal path rather than the barge, the manager told Calvin in no uncertain terms that "only those animals pulling the canal boats are allowed on the path." He neglected to inform Calvin, probably on purpose, of another road one hundred yards to the south that paralleled both the canal and the New York Central's new rail line, a vital piece of information Calvin gleaned from an idle boatman.

Missing the much-anticipated barge trip was a grave disappointment to Hiram and Sam. To lift the boys' spirits, Calvin put Hiram in charge of Barney for the trip to Buffalo and promoted Sam to assistant wagon master. Sam, envious of Hiram's new responsibility, sat at the back end of the wagon making rude comments and faces at his older brother. Hiram, in return, ran Barney up to the wagon's rear and lashed Sam a time or two with his reins. Calvin had to order Hiram off his horse and Sam out of the wagon, and he told both boys to walk alongside the wagon for an hour's punishment. "If you two continue to horse around, you'll find yourselves walking all the way to Buffalo. Understand?" he said sternly. Their behavior immediately improved.

They encountered other wagons moving west. One emigrant from White Plains, New York, driving alone in an uncovered farm wagon, told Calvin he'd heard about some new gold diggings in Colorado from his son, who'd written to say he'd dug up a fortune in a month. "I figured if that worthless kid could find himself three hundred dollars in two weeks, I could find double that amount in one week." They also encountered three scruffy, heavily armed young men in another wagon. They gave vague answers to Calvin's inquiries about their home and destination, leading Calvin to believe they were probably running from the law. Farmers, speaking a variety of languages, rode along with their families and equipment in flimsy homemade wagons and carts.

Calvin discussed with one farmer from western New York the best Missouri River town from which to depart for the plains. He said his former neighbor recommended Council Bluffs, across the river from Omaha, rather than the towns farther south like Westport. "There are some military forts near Omaha," he explained. "The soldiers ride the northern route across the plains more often than the less-used trails farther south, and it's not as long a haul from Cleveland to Council Bluffs."

Calvin had planned to take a steamer across Lake Erie from Buffalo to either Toledo or Cleveland. After that, he'd figure out a way to the Missouri River. He learned that prices were cheaper in Toledo, even though the steamer fare was more expensive, so he chose Toledo.

But there were still many overland miles to go before they reached the eastern shore of Lake Erie. Soon the boys became bored with the trip. They'd argue with each other and not pay attention to their evening chores. They'd pass hours looking through the spyglass for wild game. Sometimes they'd join Calvin in the wagon, and he'd tell them stories about the war: where he had fought, what the generals were like, and the outcomes of numerous battles. He neglected to relate his constant fear on the battlefield. Hiram wanted to know about his boyhood in New England, his schooling and how he'd managed to finish high school, his parents, and his time on a Connecticut farm. Calvin told them about things he thought had been wiped from his memory: the first book he read, a broken leg from a horse accident, his extraordinary teachers, a pet squirrel, winter sleigh rides, his aunt's cherry pies, and his loving, protective mother. He avoided talking about his alcoholic father, a mean man who'd been cruel to both Calvin and his mother.

Calvin and the boys met up with Grace and Cornelia at one of the early canal locks, where they spent a half hour trading stories about their separate journeys and searching for livestock forage. What little they found had to be supplemented by digging deeper into the grain barrel.

Calvin agreed that once Grace and Cornelia reached Buffalo, they should proceed directly to the Lake Erie steamer headed for Toledo without waiting for the rest of the family. When the wagon reached Buffalo, Calvin checked at the dock and discovered they'd missed the girls' departure by a day. The next morning, Calvin treated the boys to a hearty breakfast of eggs and bacon before they headed west to Toledo.

Ten days later, the family reunited at the dock, and Calvin loaded the girls' luggage into the wagon. Both Grace and Cornelia looked tired, with dark rings beneath their eyes after spending the night at the dock. They moved cautiously, as if unsure of each step on firm ground. Cornelia immediately headed for a mattress, where she lay motionless and silent.

Grace explained Cornelia's condition. "She's been sick almost the entire trip. Nothing stayed in her stomach, poor thing. I tried reading to calm her, but she'd cry and then vomit. The ship's captain suggested medicine that he carried, but it didn't work. Then Cornelia came down with a fever; I stayed up with her all night, fearing cholera, but the captain assured me it was only seasickness. Once ashore, he said she'd make a quick recovery. I pray that will happen."

Calvin looked at his seven-year-old daughter and then at Grace. "You've both lost considerable weight."

"We're lucky to be carrying any flesh at all, given what they fed us. Our oxen would have turned up their noses and walked away from our food. However, we did meet some very nice folks on board. One lady from New York, on her way to join her husband in Denver City, volunteered to stay up with Cornelia one evening to allow me some sleep. She gave Cornelia some medicine that relieved her vomiting during the night, but by late morning it returned after we gave her a glass of fresh milk."

THE GO-BACKER

Calvin let the girls rest for two days to take nourishment and gather strength before heading west to Council Bluffs and the Missouri River, a journey he figured would take three weeks, into mid-June, depending on the weather, everyone's health, and the stamina of the oxen.

Mid-June 1866; Council Bluffs, Iowa

The well-traveled roads across Iowa did not offer any major obstacles, and the Marlows made good time in fair weather. They did take a full day's rest to help relieve Grace's back pain. Calvin chose Council Bluffs, across the Missouri River from Omaha, Nebraska Territory's largest town, as the jumping-off spot for the journey across the plains on the Oregon Trail. The town had advertised itself, in competition with others, as providing "the cheapest and largest array of goods required on a wagon trip west." The town's shops were also well known for "mining the miners."

On their arrival, the large number of wagons headed in the opposite direction surprised Calvin. Based on the drivers' clothing and the equipment they carried, he guessed that most of the eastbound travelers were miners. The westward-bound folks called them "backsliders," as if they had lost their true religion, which was probably true for those who prayed at the altar of gold.

The Marlows lined up with other wagons at the Lone Tree Company dock, awaiting an available ferry to carry them across the river to Omaha. The ferry office wanted $4 for the wagon and another $2.50 for the livestock, plus a dollar for each person. "Of course," the ticket salesman told Calvin, "you're welcome to swim the livestock across the river. People do it. But my advice to you, sir, is to take the ferry if your oxen and horse aren't accustomed to swimmin' and doing so against a strong current. It's not for nothin' that folks call this river 'Old Misery' ... it's filled with snags, hidden sandbars, and uprooted trees, especially in the summer. If you want to take the ferry, you'll have to wait in line at least three days, judging by the crowd, before there's space available. If your critters swim, it would probably be a two-day wait for the wagon." Grace shook her head, and Calvin ponied up and paid the extra fare.

They made camp that evening in the ferry-landing lineup. Hiram gave each animal a generous grain ration while Grace cooked up a catfish she'd purchased from a fishmonger along the river. A few impatient emigrant wagons went off to another ferry landing farther south only to return late the next day to say it too was crowded.

One returnee told Calvin about the five-day wait at Nebraska City: "I counted forty-three wagons heading east. People refer to Nebraska City as 'the turntable' or 'the turnaround city.' Believe me, it's a real shithole." The helpful wagon driver and his Negro assistant offered to hold the Marlows' place in line so they could investigate the tent-and-shack town of Council Bluffs.

Not since Vermont had Calvin encountered such rutted roads, and never had he experienced a town like Council Bluffs. Bars lined the thoroughfares, offering girls, whiskey, and cards to an array of thirsty bullwhackers, mule skinners, and undisciplined soldiers who found their entertainment in beating up on equally drunk Pawnees. Outside the raucous bars and whore houses (which the soldiers referred to as 'hog farms') unattended horses, mules, oxen, and dogs filled the dusty street.

Three hours was more than enough time for Grace to spend in Council Bluffs, especially after a drunken soldier staggered into Cornelia on a garbage-laden street. To break the monotony of waiting for a ferry, she let the boys swim in the water and sit on the shore, watching a fisherman cast into the river. Grace passed the second day writing a letter to her brother.

June 17, 1866
Dear Jonathan,

Since my last letter to you, before we left Vermont, we have traveled about thirteen hundred miles, and we are now camped in Council Bluffs, Iowa, awaiting a ferry to take us across the Missouri River to Omaha in Nebraska Territory.

If not for the bank draft you sent me after the sale of mother's farm, we'd still be slaving away in the rocks of a Vermont hillside. What a mistake we made going to Vermont in the first place. Our trip west so far has been hard—not so much dangerous as physically exhausting. The never-ending days in the wagon have stiffened my back to where we had to rest for a day on the trail. I'll walk with the oxen, but it is painful at times. Poor Cornelia suffered terrible seasickness on the Lake Erie steamer, which took us from Buffalo, New York, to Toledo, Ohio. From there we have traveled west across Ohio, Indiana, Illinois, and Iowa—all excellent farm country with grain fields and orchards as far as the eye could see.

In all places, especially Illinois, the people talked about nothing else but the assassination of Mr. Lincoln. He is mourned to this day, over a year after his death. Black bunting still hangs on front porches. Had we come from the South, Illinois farmers would have blocked our passage, tarred and feathered us, and sent us on our way back home. Instead we found people friendly and helpful, with suggestions about which roads to avoid. We can buy fresh eggs, bread, and milk along the way. What a treat! We found the same friendly attitude in Iowa. What rich soil they have here! I've never seen such tall cornstalks laden with large ears.

The days pass slowly, as we are on the road at first light and make camp at dark—about thirteen to fourteen hours a day, averaging close to thirty miles on a good day, one with no rain, breakdowns, or other interruptions. I spend my days cooking, packing, unpacking, cleaning up, washing, and guiding the oxen on the rutted roads. When we rest, I read to the children. Sometimes Calvin will take the boys off hunting for prairie chickens or an occasional deer.

We were delayed getting here by a terrible rainstorm. It came down on us as if God was having a tantrum. Our delay now in crossing the river is the result of fifty-three wagons waiting in line for a ferry. The ferries from Nebraska back east to Iowa are also crowded, mostly discouraged miners and hard-luck farmers The ferries going west are packed tight with passengers and animals, like worms in a can. Just last week, one ferry caught fire in the middle of the river. Seven people drowned (including five children), and ten others saved themselves by hanging on to the ferry's burning skeleton. Downstream they are still collecting bloated animal carcasses.

This is a town of filthy drunks and bummers. I don't know when civilization will reach this depraved outpost, but it can't be soon enough for me. It will have to be emigrants like us who'll bring civilized life to the West. You can be assured it won't be the army. When and if we leave this disgraceful town, we hope to join up with a wagon train near Omaha to take us across Nebraska Territory and eventually to eastern Colorado. We've encountered some sober army troops who had been stationed at Fort Kearny, west of here, and who attest to the excellent lands in Colorado Territory, just beyond the Nebraska line along the South Platte River and on the road toward the new settlement of Denver City.

Our health is fair. It'd be better with some fresh vegetables and beef. Deer meat is a welcome and tasty change from the jerky and salt pork we carry with us. The animals too are only in fair shape. Good forage is hard to find, and what there is of it, we're forced to share with other emigrants, some of whom can get real nasty if you challenge their "right" to a patch of fresh grass.

We've met some interesting people on our journey—farmers like ourselves looking for better land, an unusual number of Mormons, who, with their handcarts, use the trail on the opposite side of the river (and from whom we keep our distance), and soldiers headed back east to muster out of the army, even a few Negroes, and I believe a fair number of outlaws. We've not encountered any highway robbers, though we heard of some in western Iowa. We've been advised to keep an eye out for those "white Indian" robbers once we're on the Oregon Trail. I'd estimate that most of the "turnarounds" are discouraged miners leaving the diggings in California or Colorado and who are now begging their way back east. The turnaround miners come under severe criticism from those headed to the mines. They are thought to be too lazy and weak-willed to mine. I guess we'd see more miners heading back home if they could afford it. I heard one miner say he'd "hang anyone who said an encouraging word about the Colorado goldfields. In a month's time, you'll see a backward stampede." Many of the miners are Irishmen who came west years ago to avoid the draft.

Everyone seems to have been hurt by the war in one way or another—financially, physically, or emotionally. A Connecticut farmer from Litchfield we met lost his two boys, killed the same day in the same battle. Another couple's crop failed, just like ours. In the evening over fires, however, the men constantly talk about the new lives they will make in the West. The optimism in their conversations keeps us determined. I call our road "The Trail of Hope."

I pray, Jonathan, that your boys are well and so too Delia. We had, as you know, a dry summer last year but a mild winter. I hope this summer brings you sufficient moisture for a large crop like those we saw between Toledo and here.

I send you my love, and will send a mailing address when we get settled, probably in three to four weeks.

Your sister,
Grace

While Grace worked on her letter, Calvin watched numerous hawkers walking along the wagon line, advertising clothing, grocery, and hardware stores in Omaha. One implement dealer's flyer advised, "Instead of mining the rocks for gold, plow the prairie for corn." A blacksmith traveled around in his cart, offering to repair broken tires and hinges, or to reshoe horses or mules. One hawker, advertising himself as a doctor, conducted a brisk trade in pills, the most popular of which guaranteed the buyer, at three dollars a capsule, the best cure for rheumatism, liver problems, lumbago, and a host of other illnesses. Another cart roamed around selling liquor, the owner advertising his whiskey as "the best 'FIREWATER' available for trade with the redskins. Take a free sip." "Muscular Missouri Mules" found eager buyers at ten dollars a head.

A middle-aged man limped along the waiting line, distributing handbills advertising himself as an experienced guide for wagons headed west. His unshaved face, with its thin-lipped mouth, never broke from a frown while his hooded, narrow eyes searched the collection of wagons for clients. He wore dirty riding boots and a filthy army campaign hat. From underneath, two ears stuck out like crow's wings. He approached Calvin as he worked on Barney's rear left foot.

"Good-lookin' Morgan stud you got there," the man said in a strong military voice.

"You've a good eye for horseflesh," Calvin responded before returning to Barney's hoof with some pliers. "I'm trying to get a piece of glass out of the hoof's frog . . . small abscess . . . been lame now for two days."

The onlooker watched closely as Calvin wiggled, pulled, and finally extracted the small glass shard from the soft tissue inside the hoof's wall.

"That'll make him feel better," Calvin said with a smile of satisfaction, but added, "I wish I had some turpentine to put on the wound."

"I got some back in my wagon," the visitor replied. "I'll be back in a jiffy."

When he returned with a pint bottle of turpentine, Calvin noticed the crossed swords insignia of the cavalry on his faded army campaign cap and the man's new pair of canvas pants held up by an army belt. Sweat stains beneath his armpits darkened the faded green cotton shirt tucked into his trousers. His cold gray eyes never fully displayed themselves through his permanent squint. Rutted lines cut through his sunburned face, which had the color and texture of a baked potato. A long purple scar ran the length of his left cheek, which suggested to Calvin a cavalry soldier who'd seen some tough service.

"A veteran of the cavalry?" Calvin asked.

"Yes sir, a company sergeant, just mustered out. Name's John Ferguson. Folks call me Johnny."

"I'm Calvin Marlow from Vermont."

"If you're from Vermont, you're sure as hell a long way from home."

Calvin nodded and expressed his impatience to get going west. He asked Johnny if he knew the country to the west.

"Know it like the back of my hand. I'm looking to put a wagon train together. I'm one short of the twenty wagons that I want to guide. Any more than twenty would only slow the progress on the trail. I have a reputation as a fast train captain. We'll move at a good steady pace from here to Fort Laramie and then on to California. Even when I guided a train that included a wagon of five prostitutes, we moved at a good clip. I only allow wagons pulled by oxen—no mules, no mares among the saddle horses, and no livestock other than those that can be ridden, led, or tied to a wagon." Then he added with emphasis, "And no wild-assed dogs."

"I'd like to join you, Johnny, but I'm headed to Colorado by way of the Denver Road at the junction of the North and South Platte Rivers."

"Not a problem," Ferguson replied. "You can join my train and leave it where the two rivers intersect and then take the Denver Road along the South Platte. Five other wagons in my train are also headed into Colorado for the gold digging near Denver City."

Calvin wanted to know what Ferguson thought of the Indian situation in northeast Colorado. "I hear there's been some Indian trouble reported near Julesburg, but that was last year. The Arapaho, Sioux, and Cheyenne attacked the fort at Julesburg in retaliation for the army's surprise attack on a hostile Indian camp at Sand Creek, Colorado. I understand things have calmed down in the Julesburg area. The army sent them Indians hightailing it into Wyoming and the Dakota Territories. And now there's a new fort outside Julesburg, Fort Sedgwick, with plenty of troops to protect the settlers and the overland travelers. Those Indians would be committing suicide if they came back. If you join my train and leave it at the Platte junction, it'd cost you fifteen dollars; it's thirty-five dollars for the trip to California. What do you say?" Calvin felt a sense of relief after hearing Ferguson's remarks, and he was comfortable with the cost, but he wanted to know more about the guide himself.

"I was born in Brooklyn to poor Irish parents who came from the old country looking for a new life. They wanted to be shopkeepers but couldn't get the money together. As for me, I found it hard to locate a job except as a sandhog or a spike pounder for the railroad. Finally, I found a job as a street cleaner, scoopin' up horse shit all day. When the draft came up, I earned me some good money as a substitute and wound up in the cavalry. I'd never been on a horse before . . . must have been all that experience with horse shit. I fought some in Virginia, and when the war ended, the army sent my unit out to Missoura on frontier duty. Been all over this country, from Texas to the Montana Territory, with different cavalry units. Finally ended up in the cavalry as a company sergeant. Retired from the army when my term expired last year. I've spent over a year out west here. I've traveled the Oregon Trail, through the Rockies, and into Oregon. Between here and there, I know where all them filthy redskins hide out. Also know how to trade with them savages and keep 'em happy . . . that's better than takin' an arrow to the chest or a tomahawk to the head." The ex-soldier paused and pointed to his cheek.

Calvin told Johnny that he'd also served in the army, and like all veterans, the two of them swapped stories about where they had served, battles they had fought, and commanders under whom they suffered.

After a few more questions, Calvin agreed to be the twentieth wagon in Ferguson's train. He received directions to the rendezvous site, a mile west of Omaha, where everyone would meet the day after they crossed the river. In the meantime, Ferguson said he'd be "getting myself between the soft thighs of a young woman I met in town a couple of days ago. You won't find many cherries between here and the new mining towns in Colorado, so it's a long way between fucks. I'd advise you to get what you need right here in Council Bluffs." Ferguson gave Calvin directions to what he considered the best hog farm in town and described its extraordinary range of prices.

Calvin looked at Ferguson and said in a stern voice, "I don't much appreciate your language. I have a wife." He then added, "I trust we are riding with a trail guide, not a whoremaster."

Ferguson apologized and asked about the family. When he learned the family included children, he asked their ages. "Well behaved? We can't be runnin' after children all along the trail." Calvin assured him they were well behaved. *What about you, Ferguson?* he thought but didn't ask. *Are you well behaved?* Instead, he asked what Ferguson thought about the numerous wagons headed in the opposite direction.

"Mostly a bunch of dumb, lazy miners. Couldn't find their ass with both hands. A few are loaded with gold dust. You can pick them out . . . the ones with a smile, packin' pistols and Sharp rifles. Them glum ones only found some mule shit, packed up, and headed back this way. I call 'em the go-backers. I'll guess for every ten who have gone to the mines to see the elephant, nine are headed back to where they came from if they have the means to do so." Having dismissed the group summarily, Ferguson turned and called over his shoulder, "See you at daylight day after tomorrow, Calvin."

Late the next afternoon, the Marlows loaded the wagon onto the ferry. Cornelia broke into uncontrollable tears when confronted with the prospect of the river crossing. Grace calmed her during the thirty-minute passage by holding her tight against her chest and directing her attention to the freight barges beached on the opposite shore.

Grace observed that Omaha differed little from Council Bluffs with its collection of tents, shacks, and warehouses crowded around the dock, arranged in little semblance of order. Gangs of Union Pacific railroad laborers—Negroes, Anglos, Indians, and Asians—unloaded cattle, rails, and ties from the barges onto freight wagons. The cattle were destined for the town's new slaughterhouses, and the rails and ties were headed for the new railroad line on the western outskirts of Omaha.

Grace asked Calvin about Ferguson, the guide he had talked with in Council Bluffs. He told her, "I judge him to be an experienced cavalry sergeant but without much religion. He claims to know the trails and how to avoid Indians along the way. He wants to be our captain, the same as a trail boss, which is fine by me given his experience and knowledge of the country." Calvin then returned to checking the canvas bonnet and coated it with another application of linseed oil and beeswax. "How are we doing on provisions?" he asked Grace.

"We could sure use a bag of flour, some fresh meat, and fresh eggs if they're available," Grace replied, almost pleading.

"I need some more grain for Barney. Once I get him reshod, I'll see what I can find."

The next morning, nineteen wagons assembled at the designated spot west of town, all impatiently awaiting the twentieth, which arrived ten minutes late.

"If you're goin' to join this wagon train, you'll learn to be on time, mister," Ferguson admonished the head of the newly arrived family.

The scruffy driver looked at Ferguson and barked back, "Who the hell are you to be timing my arrival?"

"Mister, I'm attempting to put a wagon train together. And to be a member, timeliness is required of everyone, including children," Ferguson responded in a firm voice accompanied by a harsh stare. "If you want to join this train, get your ass over here."

Ferguson then turned his attention to the crowd of emigrants gathered around him. "The first order of business is to elect a captain and deputy captain for this wagon train. The captain serves as train boss, which is the usual arrangement for almost all trains moving west. I'd like to be your captain." Ferguson went on to detail his experience, including his recent service as a company sergeant in a cavalry regiment. "I know this here Oregon Trail like the palm of my hand: where to cross rivers, where to make camp and which sites to avoid, where to find game, and how to deal with any redskins we might encounter. I've also picked up some medical training in the army. My fee is thirty-five dollars for a wagon headed to California or Oregon and fifteen dollars for a wagon leaving the train at the intersection of the two Platte rivers in western Nebraska." After his short speech, silence fell among the crowd.

Then one man raised his hand and asked, "Who can vouch for your character?" No one spoke up. Finally, Ferguson responded: "I have with me my honorable discharge papers, signed by General Custer, and an accompanying Certificate of Outstanding Service signed by the general." He dug in his leather pouch, unfolded the documents, and passed them to his questioner, who handed them to someone who could read. The man read the certificate to the assembled wagon masters and said to the anxious crowd, "Looks good to me." Another man raised his hand and announced, "I nominate Mr. Ferguson to be our wagon captain. One vote per wagon."

Ferguson counted nineteen raised hands and one abstention—the dour latecomer, who clearly thought Ferguson too cocky, if not arrogant. Then the new wagon captain stood amid the emigrants and thanked them for their confidence. He turned to Calvin and said to the crowd, "I'd like to nominate Mr. Calvin Marlow as my deputy captain. He's a Vermont Yankee and a veteran like me, with a distinguished record." Without discussion or even time for Calvin to decline the nomination, a unanimous vote elected the new deputy captain, again with one abstention.

Ferguson stepped forward, shook Calvin's hand, and proceeded with his announcements.

"Marlow will soon appoint his two deputies. Now before we start off, I want you to know that everyone's safety comes first. We must, therefore, set some rules that I expect everyone to follow while we're on the trail. Like an army unit, we need to be a disciplined team, to assist each other when there's an injury, an accident, or illness. Cooperation is critical when we cross rivers and in the event a wagon gets mired in mud or quicksand.

"We will line up and be ready to move at daylight. Keep an interval between wagons of no more and no less than five yards, or fifteen feet. Notice that all our wagons are pulled by oxen; no mules, horses, or cattle, 'cept for those ridden or roped to a wagon. Wagon trains under my direction are known for their quick pace, which in some cases may affect your personal comfort. But the less time we're on the trail, the fewer opportunities the Indians will have to locate us. If we maintain a steady pace, we should make two to three miles an hour on the trail and, with stops, at least twenty miles a day, or a minimum of one hundred miles a week. We'll rest on the Sabbath.

"Don't be surprised by the number of wagons on the trail. It's still less than last year due to the rumors of Indian troubles in small isolated areas in Montana. Remember, we can only travel as fast as the slowest wagon. We won't have time to wait for children who have wandered off. Keep all weapons empty and close by in your wagon. I will tell you when weapons should be loaded and then half-cocked for safety. If water's available, we'll take a midmorning water break. All the traffic on the trail has caused some deep ruts and washes. Try and avoid 'em.

"At midday, during the heat of the day, we'll take another break to rest ourselves, have a snack and water, and graze our livestock. Be careful to avoid water with crawlies or a salty taste, which means it has alkali in it. It can kill livestock as quick as lightning.

"For your wagons, keep your spokes, hounds, and hubs moist. They'll dry out fast in the hot weather. Check your tires often; if they loosen, hammer in some wooden shims. Also remember to properly secure your canvas covers and keep them oiled with a thin coating of tallow. Sure as hell we'll run into some nasty storms . . . you can count on some hail.

"At the end of the day's march, we will arrange our wagons in a circle to form a corral, starting with my wagon and leaving an opening halfway around the circle, or after the tenth wagon, for livestock to enter and exit the interior circle, where our oxen and saddle horses will graze. When you hear the order 'Drive up,' the wagon masters will assist the night guards in corralling the oxen into the center of the circle. Two men will be posted every evening to guard all other livestock—cattle and horses— grazing away from our camp; another man will serve as guard in and around our corral. Be sure to picket your livestock that might run off from the grazing herd. We won't have time to round up stray cattle. Remember, the care and safety of your livestock must be your primary concern. Let me worry about the route and all those details. Without healthy livestock, you'll be alone out here on the plains with every hardship it has to offer. And believe me, it has plenty to offer.

"I also need to mention the wind. It can gust to over seventy miles an hour, and when it does and we're headed directly into it, the wind can whip through your wagon and tear off the bonnet. Best thing to do is put your wagon sideways to the wind and anchor it with a rope tied either to a tree or a spike in the ground.

"And one other matter. The day of the Sabbath will be a rest day." Ferguson stopped and took a swig from a canteen. The emigrants sat silent, looking around at one another with serious stares.

The captain continued. "We can expect a fair amount of traffic on the trail now, with the war ended. I'll select the campsite each evening when the sky ain't got much light in it, somewhere close to water and forage for the livestock. The next day I want those campsites left clean. Nothin' worse than pullin' into a campsite that looks and smells like a dump, with flies buzzin' everywhere, unburied garbage, and bears sniffin' about. I'll tell you when it is safe enough to have fires for cookin'. If there are fires, be careful of sparks. One of them can light a canvas covering in a second, and before you can get to your water jug, your wagon is afire. Kill all fires dead after supper. You can have morning fires, but remember, we're on the road at daybreak. For reveille, the guard will fire off a shotgun blast an hour before sunrise. You'll have time for breakfast before lining up in formation behind me.

"Now regarding any Indians we may encounter, there will be more and more beggars on the road with the decline in the number of buffalo. The beggars will be lookin' for sugar, coffee, flour, liquor, blankets, or sometimes a trinket of some sort. If not beggars, and depending on the tribe, the Indians may demand a tribute for passing through what they consider to be their tribal land. They may want to trade hides for those items, but in most cases they just want to take, with no give in return. Also, we don't trade weapons, liquor, or women with Indians. Let me do the talkin'. Under no circumstances should you fire a weapon at them unless provoked. It will only cause retaliation and an attack. At night, our livestock guards will call for assistance by firing two shots. Their calls for help will usually be caused by Indians, most likely Sioux, attempting to steal or stampede our livestock. Any questions?"

From the back of the assembled gathering came a question from a young woman. "If we have an emergency while traveling on the trail and we need to stop, what do we do?"

"Pull off to the side of the trail and send a rider or a runner to me at the head of the train, where I will always be with my wagon. I'll halt the train. But remember, long stoppages can be dangerous, so be damned quick to return to the train. Any other questions?"

A wagon master asked, "Who will post the guards?"

"I will, and I shall attempt to even out the postings so that every man carries an equal responsibility. I'll also change the wagon line order so that everyone shares equally the tail-end dust."

"Why no loaded weapons in the wagons?" came a question from the front row.

"I've seen too many accidents, even among experienced soldiers. Obviously, if a fight breaks out with Indians, you don't need permission to load weapons and defend yourselves. But when traveling where I know there are no redskins, there's no need to be bouncing around with loaded weapons.

"One other matter: I will want to know about all accidents, sickness, and serious animal problems you have on the trail. Remember, we work as a team. I want every wagon master to sign up on this here roster. Include family members and number of saddle horses and other livestock you are traveling with. Mr. Marlow here will assist anyone who has difficulty with his

THE GO-BACKER

writing. Shortly, we'll practice forming the circle that we'll use at day's end. I'll be the first wagon; the next wagon will back itself so that its right rear touches the left front of my wagon. All tongues will be turned to the outside so as to ease the task of unhitching and hitching your teams. After chaining to the wagon to your front, unhitch your team and lead them off to the side to allow the next wagon to repeat the process. It will take some practice to get it right. Maintain a five-yard interval between the tenth and eleventh wagon to allow livestock to enter and exit inside the makeshift corral when necessary."

After the wagon owners signed the roster, all the families returned to their wagons and then . . . mass confusion. The sound of snapping whips, yells, and shouts filled the air as Ferguson ran back and forth, cursing while issuing orders to the wagon masters maneuvering through the dust. After thirty minutes, the corral circle had formed, though not as perfectly or as quickly as Ferguson had hoped. Most of the problems arose from teams unaccustomed to backing up with precision.

"Not bad for the first time. It'll come easier next time. Don't forget the break between the tenth and eleventh wagon. Also, a little less shouting will keep the animals calm and more manageable. Use the afternoon to get some rest and make any needed repairs to your wagons. I notice that some of the teams need practice backing up their wagons. The circle will break at first light, and we'll be on our way to gold and a new life."

Cheers went up.

"Oh, I forgot one thing," Ferguson said as he raised his hand to quiet the crowd. "On the trail, when nature calls, men go off to the right and women to the left. If we're in open country, use your chamber pots. They can be emptied and the contents buried at our evening campsite. Again, I want those sites left clean for other travelers on the trail."

June 1866, Nebraska Territory

Disassembling the wagon circle the next morning came easier to the emigrants than forming it the day before. Still, the sun was an hour high by the time the wagons lined up behind Ferguson. But once they were moving and on the trail, the captain appeared pleased with the skill of the drivers as they maintained a steady pace with the proper intervals. One wagon had to stop briefly to adjust a yoke, and another wagon's load shifted and had to be reassembled, but other than that, there were no delays.

During the midmorning water break, Ferguson asked Calvin to ride with him. "There are some details I want to go over with you and a few other issues." Calvin explained that he needed to give Grace some more lessons and practice with handling the oxen before he felt comfortable leaving the team to her. "How about tomorrow?" Ferguson suggested.

"That would work," Calvin responded without much enthusiasm. He wasn't in the mood to listen to any more of Ferguson's sexual escapades.

Grace's handling of the oxen the next day demonstrated to Calvin that she could control the team while walking beside the oxen with a whip or by sitting in the wagon seat shouting commands and snapping the reins. During the midday break, Calvin jumped up on Ferguson's wagon. Inside, he noticed a mattress bed with an army blanket, over which hung a holstered pistol and a scabbard with a rifle. A camp chair, table, small cookstove, campaign chest, and four barrels took up the floor space, leaving a small area for a hunting dog chained to an eyebolt.

He congratulated the captain on his comfortable wagon and sat down in the jockey seat next to him.

Ferguson said he liked to travel in a comfortable and civilized style. He then pointed to the barrels and identified them. "In that barrel I got me some good whiskey, for medicinal purposes, of course." Ferguson gave a wide smile, unusual for him. Pointing to another barrel, he said, "There, I got some trade items for the savages. How they do love them blankets and trinkets." The captain continued, pointing to the English hound dog. "That there dog about eats me out of all the food I carry for him. But he's worth it. Good company, and has a nose on him that can flush out a hidden redskin, a covey of quail, or, even better, some prairie chickens. How you gettin' along?"

"No problems," Calvin responded. "Grace is comfortable driving the oxen and is teaching my oldest boy how to handle the animals, either on foot or from the jockey box. Kid's a fast learner and as stout as they come," he added.

"Like father, like son, they say. Now, Calvin, I want to go over a few things. There's been a nasty outbreak of cholera along this trail for the last year or so. Where it's come from, I can only guess. It may have come from the army, who passed it on to the redskins and the emigrants traveling the trail. I didn't want to mention it in front everyone yesterday, but it is a serious matter. Doctors tell me it is caused by a germ that enters the body through the mouth and infects the intestines, causing dehydration, severe diarrhea, and vomiting. Hell, one doesn't need a guide to follow this trail west. All you need to do is to follow them grave markers. There must be over a hundred of them between here and Fort Kearny. Another concern of mine is the unpredictability of the Indians.

"You never know what the redskins will do. A lot of it has to do with the character of the specific tribe . . . Sioux, Arapaho, Cheyenne, or Pawnee. They can be as friendly as a missionary priest and the best of guides one day; the next day, without warning, a different tribe will attack for some unknown reason and take your scalp. They're hard to figure. So we need to be careful not to misinterpret what for them may be a friendly gesture as an aggressive move . . . or the reverse. I've had some experience with them, so let me do the talkin'.

"I do know that when the army is patrolling in their area, they can be ornery as hell. I have to admit, too often it's the army that starts trouble. As far as I can tell, all them Indians want is to be left alone so they can hunt the buffalo. But the army won't let them alone. Hell, the cavalry ain't got no one else to fight now that Johnny Reb has surrendered. And how's an officer to get promoted if he can't take on some redskins and then write up an exaggerated report to Washington about how he and his troops saved the West from the savages? I hear Custer exaggerated his reports a couple of times in the Civil War. Write it up and presto, a promotion from colonel to general."

"You served under Custer, right?" Calvin asked.

"Unfortunately, yes. Now there's an example of what I'm talking about. That son of a bitch has caused more trouble out here in the West than he's worth. I'd have liked to piss in his whiskey."

Calvin responded, "He sure gained a good reputation in the war and since."

"Yeah, but he's hell on his troopers. I got myself in real trouble with Long Hair. That's why I'm no longer a cavalryman."

"In what way?" Calvin asked.

"I'll tell you the story if you keep it confidential," replied Ferguson. Calvin agreed.

"Up in the Dakotas in the spring of this year, we made camp about twenty miles west of Fort McKeen. Our mission was to hunt down some Sioux who had reportedly attacked some emigrant wagon trains farther west. Within our ranks we had five troopers down with 'putrid throat,' what you call diphtheria. The regimental doctor, without the proper medicine to control diphtheria, feared an outbreak throughout the regiment of the contagious disease. One day in the early afternoon, when we were camped, Custer announced to the regimental sergeant that he'd ride back to Fort McKeen and find the proper medicine. Refusing to be accompanied by guards, he announced, 'I'll be back before supper,' and took off, heading east with his hunting dogs, a carbine, and a shotgun. By supper, Custer was nowhere to be seen; at daybreak the next morning, he was still absent. My company commander selected three troopers, one of them my brother, to ride out and search for Custer. An hour later, the search party returned to camp to report that a small Indian hunting party of well-armed braves attacked them and killed my brother. We later discovered that the savages had scalped my brother and had run off with his clothing and weapons . . . a pistol, a carbine, and a knife.

"Later that morning, who shows up but Custer with a huge buck tied to the back of his horse and a wide smile on his dusty face. As he dismounted, he ordered a nearby private to take the buck and dress it out. Custer explained his absence by saying he'd lost his bearings on the flat prairie landscape so he'd made camp in a dry wash the previous evening. 'I never did find my way to Fort McKeen. Good thing I got lost,' Custer said cheerfully, 'or I'd have never seen that beautiful buck I brought down with one well-aimed shot early this morning.'

"The dumb-ass general never did explain how he'd lost his bearings yesterday but somehow found them today. A junior officer came up to Custer and said something to him in private. Custer's countenance changed from a joyful smile to a serious frown. I doubt if that son of a bitch felt any sense of remorse for causing the death of my brother by taking leave of his command for his personal pleasure."

Ferguson took a long swig from his canteen, which to Calvin smelled suspiciously like whiskey, and continued, "A couple of months later, back at Fort Riley, Kansas, our winter quarters, I was summoned to Custer's very comfortable residence where I was greeted warmly by the general and his attractive wife. After a cup of tea, Custer directed me to his small office where I took a seat in front of his desk, which was covered with maps and documents. His aide-de-camp stood nearby. Custer briskly dismissed the aide and then looked directly at me and announced, 'Ferguson, I think you need to leave the army immediately.' I stood mute. Then, to break the silence, Custer held up a document and declared, 'I have here a copy of a letter you wrote in November of last year to General Sherman and the army adjutant general's office in Washington. In it, you make some serious, unfounded changes against my actions as your commander. Because of your letter, I am now under investigation by the army. If you agree to resign, I will see to it that you receive one hundred and fifty dollars in specie and an award for your outstanding service to the army.' Then Custer held up the beautiful certificate, which he had prepared but not signed. I asked for time to think over the proposition. 'Captain Ferguson,' Custer responded, 'you need to think seriously about my offer.' If I didn't resign, Custer let me know he'd sure as hell make life difficult for me. He gave no specifics, but I could guess. He stood up from his desk and said he'd see me there tomorrow at the same time.

"I showed up at the general's quarters the next day, and he greeted me warmly, but with no offer of tea. In his study, he asked, 'Do you have an answer to my proposition?' I'd given considerable thought to the general's bribe. I didn't see any bright future for myself in the army, especially if the general remained my commanding officer. Plus, the offer of one hundred and fifty dollars in hard currency was equal to almost nine months of pay. 'I accept your kind offer, sir,' I blurted out while I thought of my dead brother. Custer signed the certificate, rolled it up, secured it with a yellow ribbon, and then handed me the gold coins from a small leather pouch. I thanked the general, and with neither of us having any more to say to each other, I saluted him before I departed his office. At the front door, Mrs. Custer smiled at me as I exited. Once out of the army, I never heard from Custer or the army adjutant general's office.

"I did discover a while back from a soldier I met at Fort Riley and who served in the adjutant general's Washington office that Custer admitted in an affidavit that he had left his command without authority, not to go hunting as I reported, but to ride to Fort McKeen where he could secure medicine for some sick troopers under his command. They must have dropped the investigation and the idea of a court-martial, because the general remains in command to this day. So, Marlow, here I am leading you across the plains and not too far away from where Custer bagged a buck."

Calvin sat astounded at Ferguson's story. After the war, he'd heard of Custer's success and bravery as a young officer in combat, how he frequently caught Johnny Reb with his pants down, and how, in reports to senior officers, he exaggerated his own role so as to grow and protect his reputation. Calvin hadn't realized the extent to which Custer had lied.

The white-bonneted prairie train pushed westward along the North Platte toward Fort Kearny without incident. One morning, a young boy, Aaron Blakely, came running up to Ferguson's lead wagon and shouted for help with his mother. "Her fever is worse, sir. Can you attend to her?" The emigrants all knew it had to be the wagon that had reported a case of cholera immediately after their departure from Council Bluffs, a town known for its bad water.

Ferguson halted the train and walked with the boy to his wagon. On the way, he stopped to ask Calvin if Grace might help with the cholera case. Ferguson explained, "She'll need to be cleaned head to foot, and it wouldn't be appropriate for me to undress her." The captain, Grace, and Calvin followed the Blakely boy to the wagon. His mother had retched all over her blanket, and the sour smell of vomit and green excrement filled the air. Her husband sat close to her on the mattress, mopping her forehead with a wet towel. "Nothing seems to comfort her," he complained to Ferguson. With her eyes shrunk back in their dark sockets, her weak response to a question from the captain vanished in the wagon's foul interior.

Ferguson asked the husband where and when he had last filled his water barrels. When James Blakely responded, "Omaha," the captain ordered him to empty all the water barrels, refill them at the river, and bring back some floating ice, if you see some. Meanwhile, Grace had stripped Sarah Blakely of her fouled clothing, washed her clean, and fashioned a pair of diapers from a cotton sheet. When James and Aaron returned from the river with two barrels of fresh water and a chunk of ice, Ferguson told the husband, "There's little I can do for cholera except to advise you to keep the missus drinkin' tepid water . . . a quart in the morning and another in the afternoon. Also, in the early evening, boil up some water with a few slices of beef jerky and a dried green vegetable. Let her sip the broth slowly for nourishment, and maybe that will stop her squirts."

On the way back to their wagons, the captain said to Grace, "I do want to thank you for your help with a very unpleasant task. I wish there was more I could do, but there's no known effective cure for cholera. I'll be surprised if she makes it another day." He then added an aside to Calvin: "Join me up at my wagon, would you?"

At the lead wagon, Calvin took the reins from Ferguson while he pulled the remnants of a slaughtered deer from a sack and threw it at his dog. Then the captain turned to Calvin.

"We should be at Fort Kearny by late tomorrow if we don't have no more delays. I fear the cholera lady won't make it."

That evening over a cook fire adjacent to the wagon circle, young Blakely ran to the captain and said his mother was unconscious. Ferguson and Calvin hurried with the boy to his wagon. James sat on the mattress, pressing an ice pack to Sarah's forehead, but her eyes were closed and her hands were clasped on her chest, with no visible sign of life. After feeling Sarah's wrist and throat, the captain said quietly, "Can't find a pulse." And then he added, as if he were a preacher, "God has taken her to his house." The young boy screamed, and his father raised himself to his knees, leaned over the shrunken body, and kissed his dead wife's forehead. "I'd like a minute to be with her alone," he said softly as the others jumped from the wagon.

The captain tried to control the hysterical boy, but without success. He turned to Calvin for assistance. Calvin said he'd have Grace prepare Sarah for burial and suggested that she be taken to Fort Kearny. "They have burial grounds on military posts."

The captain responded quickly, "You should know the army don't want a cholera corpse in or near a post. And if they discovered that we'd been carrying a cholera corpse with us, they'd never allow us to camp at the fort. We must bury her here tonight."

"Shouldn't we ask James?" Calvin suggested.

"I don't care what the hell he says. She's goin' to be buried tonight . . . right here," Ferguson replied as he pointed to where some of the men were digging a fire pit.

The captain and Calvin went off to talk with the widowed husband, and together they laid out a plan. The captain made it very plain that a burial at Fort Kearny was out of the question. "When everyone has turned in for the night, we'll dig a grave right where the fire is and then cover the grave with ashes. It'll keep any animals or Indians from finding the grave. Take my word for it, them redskins are grave robbers . . . lookin' for clothes or valuables."

Grace hid her disagreeable task from the other train members and prepared the corpse for burial. Meanwhile, James and Calvin carefully removed the ashes from the fire pit and dug a deep grave into the soft ground. Ferguson could find no materials with which to make a rough casket and said, to no one in particular, "She'll have to be buried Indian style." That night, with only the three men in attendance, the captain read a prayer and the grieving husband placed the last shovelful of sand on the grave, the most recent of many on the Oregon Trail.

Calvin joined the captain at his wagon for a whiskey nightcap.

"Can't wait to get to the fort tomorrow," the captain said as he took a healthy slug from his jug. "If I know my army, they'll have some nice wet pussies there for the soldiers, particularly for them officers, not to mention passing emigrants. The first sergeant at a post like Fort Kearny is expected to act like a pimp for extra income. Hell, I made sixty dollars in one month at Fort Riley. Them troopers would line up for miles to get some pussy. Custer allowed it, in fact he participated at least once that I know of. He'd use those Indian girls we captured, or them young white Irish girls who'd come out from the East

Coast, following the soldiers and their money west. I remember one girl, a cute blonde with tits the size of two frying pans. She had married one of our officers and then hired herself out as a washerwoman. Some of those washerwomen could put starch in your pecker, and for a quarter you could spend a night with one of them rolling around in the laundry room atop a pile of dirty clothes. Hell, those washerwomen, wherever I was stationed, were nothing more than prostitutes . . . some of them could actually wash clothes and iron, but that'd be an exception. They'd pass on the clap. That's why the regimental surgeon ordered all of them to come in for an inspection. How they passed, I can only guess. I'm sure them surgeons took in some extra money also. It's real expensive living on the army frontier, but it won't show up in any of the accounts."

"You say that Custer participated? I thought you said he was married," Calvin asked.

"He was married last I knew. I met his wife, a very nice lady. But I do know he bedded one of them New York girls. She told me confidentially she'd serviced the colonel. 'His hair kept getting in my face; at first he rode me like a horse in a slow trot, but once he got himself going, he moved into a hard-charging gallop. Good thing he wasn't wearing his fucking spurs.' Them were tough girls. Olive oil was their lubricant of choice when they could find it, and I don't mean for their salad. I always brought them a bottle of that oil. Got some over in that crate."

"Besides all the wonderful sexual adventures the post has to offer, what else can we expect?" Calvin asked.

"Them merchants at the fort will have the best provisions this side of Fort Laramie. 'Bout everything you want: grain, flour, sugar, even fresh meat and eggs, segars, and jugs of Missouri liquor. But their prices will kill you . . . merchants know exactly what we travelers want and need. Also, you'll see some inferior food for sale that was destined for the Indians as rations. Them merchants got paid by the government for the food, that never did get to the Indians, and now they're selling it a second time. Don't touch it. It's rotten and moldy.

"At another store they sell things the troopers found discarded on the trail. I once saw a beautiful organ and a couple of small pianos. Another thing to remember, you'll want to be sleeping in your wagon, not in one of them 'dobe buildings that make up the fort. That 'dobe is home to bugs, worms, and them fuckin' prairie rattlers. They're mean little sons of bitches; they can kill a human and lame up a horse or ox real bad."

Late the next day, after a somber ride across the prairie, Calvin caught sight of the fort's stockade on an embankment before he saw the complex of buildings. Teamsters and soldiers unloaded freight in front of an adobe warehouse. In the distance, everyone in the train could hear cannon fire. "Just practice," Calvin assured Grace.

Once at the fort, the captain announced that there'd be no need for a wagon circle that evening. He also announced that the next day would be a day of rest and for everyone to take advantage of the time to replenish supplies. Calvin fed an extra grain ration to the oxen and then made a tour of the fort with his boys. Meanwhile, Grace wrote to her brother.

June 27, 1866
Dear Jonathan,

We have just today arrived at Fort Kearny. The fort is crowded with travelers like ourselves, this place being the merging point for three trails: ours from Omaha, another from Nebraska City, and a third from St. Joseph, Missouri. A soldier here told us that 60 wagons a week pass through the fort. We are about halfway to Colorado, and already ten days on the trail from Omaha, where I last wrote you. How lovely it is to have a day of rest and not be bouncing around in the wagon and keeping the two youngest occupied.

You can't imagine how crowded this trail is. Right after we started off from Omaha, we kept running up against freighters and Mormons crowding the trail with their handcarts. We then crossed the Platte River with some difficulty to the south side, where our captain thought it would be less crowded. No handcarts on the south side but plenty of other wagon trains, columns of infantry and cavalry with their supply wagons, and the ever-present freighters. They're a mean lot, those bullwhackers. They won't move to let us pass, and when we do they let out a string of oaths unfamiliar even to an army veteran like Calvin.

And what a relief it is to be here, guarded from sandstorms and taking a day or so to rest. I look forward to the luxury of hot meals, puddings, and delicious fruit pies; I understand fresh eggs are also available! All is quiet here except that we encountered twelve armed soldiers a mile east of the fort, riding out looking to recover ten army horses stolen two nights ago by an Indian raiding party.

Poor Calvin has taken on the added responsibility of train sub-captain after he was elected by the wagon masters. He has served diligently and is very well respected among all in our train. His eye is always on the trail, looking for obstacles; rarely does he lift his head to look around and appreciate the scenery. It can be beautiful, especially at dusk. As train sub-captain, Calvin must often be absent from our wagon, which puts more responsibility on the rest of us.

Hiram is a great help to Calvin and me. He can now guide the oxen team on foot and is learning quickly how to drive them with reins from the jockey seat. He and Sam together can hitch and unhitch the team. Hiram must boost Sam to the top of one ox to secure the yoke, and then Sam jumps over to the other animal to repeat the process. Very funny to watch the two of them. Cornelia will sometimes join me when I'm driving the wagon from afoot. She's learned to snap a whip with the best of those bullwhackers.

On Sundays, when we rest, all the team members circle around for a prayer meeting. Afterward, Cornelia helps me with the washing and cooking while Calvin joins the boys hunting or makes repairs to the wagon.

We've had no troubles on our trip, though we have had numerous delays. We've had to stop for broken wheels or axles and sore-footed oxen. Only one tragedy so far. The wife of one of our train members from Pennsylvania died of cholera last night. Our wagon captain tried everything to save her, but in vain. I prepared her for burial, something I had never done before and hope never to do again. Our wagon captain is very helpful, much better than I had anticipated. He knows his way and selects good campsites away from other wagon trains and distant from any Indians. Thank God, we have not seen any redskins so far. The captain does, however, on occasion make me feel uncomfortable. As others have confirmed, he does have an eye for the women.

Despite all the grumbling from the wagon masters about the captain's fast rate of travel, his guard assignments, and the short midday breaks, we are all pleased to be making good progress toward western destinations. Like others before us, some of our wagons have lightened their loads. You'd be surprised how much is discarded on the trail. Other wagon trains have discarded pianos, oak chests, cookstoves, a lovely loom, and a wagon, now just a skeleton, having been stripped of its useful parts. Calvin wanted to recover a large grindstone, but we couldn't find room for it. I had my eye on a lovely butter churn, but Calvin asked me where I'd find the cream. We are told by the fort commander that in the last twelve months approximately twenty-two thousand emigrants have passed the fort on the Oregon Trail.

We encountered one wagon the other day headed toward us from the west. The owner had picked up discarded items along the trail—horseshoes, chests, empty oak barrels, a couple of poorly tanned buffalo robes, large scraps of canvas, a wagon axle, an oak tongue, and pine floorboards—all for sale. We passed another wagon piled high with buffalo bones, to be sold for fertilizer back in Omaha for five dollars a ton.

I do tire of our food. There is not much variety to it. I'm hoping we can buy some fresh vegetables here at the fort and maybe some fresh meat. I've not had an egg in weeks.

Not much time for socializing. If I'm not washing or mending clothes or cooking, I'm leading or driving the wagon while Calvin and the boys are hunting or gathering wood, twigs, dead sage, or buffalo chips for our fires. Each day west, it is more difficult to find fuel for our fires. The chips make good fuel, but they do have an unpleasant acid odor, which I seem unable to wash from my hair. I much prefer to eat the animals than smell them! For relief, I rub sagebrush into my hair. Calvin says I smell like the prairie. "Better that than a buffalo," I always say.

Three days ago, Calvin saw off in the distance a dead buffalo with arrows in its flank and a pool of blood underneath its mouth. But when he went to investigate it, he noticed two Indians hiding behind a bluff. The whinny of Calvin's horse quickly confirmed their presence. Calvin made a quick retreat. The captain said the Indians use the buffalo to lure soldiers or emigrants for a quick kill. Smart devils they are!

The wildflowers are spread across the open meadows. We see tiger lilies, lady's slippers, silver sage, mallow, indigo, and milkweed. Among the birds are meadowlarks, quail, sage hens, hawks, redwinged blackbirds, and some I can't identify. There is a wide variety of animals: fox, badgers, gophers, coyotes, deer, wolves, and buffalo almost every day. The wolves leave us alone. They're more interested in hunting down an old bull buffalo, a weak fawn, or a jackrabbit than encountering a shotgun blast from Calvin. Besides disease, especially cholera, our most deadly enemy here is the rattlesnake, and now that we are on the prairie, they are very common. Because of them, the captain says to surround the children at night with a lariat laid on the ground around them. He tells us a rattler won't crawl over a lariat. I don't believe it, so I have the children crowd inside with us every evening. Before bedtime every night, I must inspect them for sandburs.

I did recently encounter an unusual sight. What I thought at first to be a large eagle's nest turned *out to be an Indian-built scaffold high in a tree, on which they had placed a corpse wrapped in a white blanket and a buffalo robe. At the foot of the tree were some horse bones. The captain told us this was the traditional Indian way by which to send a warrior to his future life. The buzzards surely had a feast. Terrible!*

After we depart here, we'll leave the main wagon train in about a week and head down the South Platte Road into Colorado Territory, near the small community of Julesburg. It is reportedly excellent farming ground and safe from Indians, with a sizable number of troops at Fort Sedgwick nearby. We believe the grain crops from our new homestead will find a ready market for those headed up the Bozeman Trail into Montana.

One major annoyance on the trail is the giant horseflies. Calvin says if he could catch one, he'd put a saddle on it and fly off to Julesburg, and give it a look from the air. Maybe a cloud of flies could take our entire family to Julesburg. How I wish!

Thank God, we are all in good health.

Write when you can and bring me current with your family. You can address us at Fort McPherson, Colorado Territory.

Don't worry about us, though you could say a prayer for us from time to time.

We all send you much love and our prayers.
Grace

Late June 1866, Nebraska Territory

The layover improved everyone's mood, except for one wagon driver, who complained to the captain that he'd spent more days sucking dust at the end of the train than anyone else. The captain said he'd check his records, "but in the meantime, you line up tomorrow right behind me." Another wagon reported a young child with "camp fever," but the fort doctor ruled out cholera and said the boy's infected foot had caused the fever.

Calvin had asked three different soldiers about the safety of the Julesburg area. They all reported it safe, though they did mention small, intermittent Indian raids from time to time between Fort Kearny and the South Platte Road to Julesburg, but nothing to be concerned about. One junior officer judged eastern Colorado "a superb farming area with excellent grass for livestock and water from the South Platte." "That's where I'd like to settle after my retirement," he told Calvin. "It is more peaceful now that the army has moved more troops into Fort Sedgwick and also another army post, Fort Morgan, upriver one hundred miles. They've strengthened the breastworks by heightening and thickening the walls and enlarged the accommodations for the infantry and cavalry who continue to guard the railroad crews, the Pikes Peak Express Company's mail coaches, stages, and supply trains along the trail."

After a full day at Fort Kearny, the wagon train pulled out at daybreak with all members rested and in good spirits. Calvin asked the captain if he had enjoyed his rest. "Didn't find me anything halfway attractive," the captain replied with a deep frown. "Mostly fat old bitches demanding a month's salary for a roll in a filthy bed. I don't know how those soldiers survive. The first sergeant told me the post commander runs the place like a nunnery. Damn, I sure need myself a good fuck... somethin' better than what Kearny had to offer."

"I hear Fort Laramie is a real hot spot for 'pretties,'" Calvin answered in an attempt to humor the captain.

"Sure hope so, I do. Can't wait to get there to find me some fallen doves—at a fair price, of course."

On the second day out from Fort Kearny and during the midday break with oxen unhitched, a band of ten mounted and armed Indian braves suddenly appeared on the trail ahead. They walked their horses slowly toward the wagons, but not in an aggressive manner.

"Indians," one wagon master cried out.

"Quiet," the captain shouted as he stepped forward and gave a friendly greeting—arm half raised, with the palm of the hand facing the armed Indians. As the captain approached on foot, the Indian leader, identified by a dirty army officer's jacket and a motley feather headdress, returned the friendly sign. He indicated his tribal affiliation by drawing his hand across his throat—a Sioux. The pantomime continued, and after a few minutes, the captain turned away from the Indian and walked to his wagon. He returned with a small roll of thin copper wire and a white blanket.

After Ferguson offered the items to the Indian, the warrior made a motion of wanting more and then said, "Liquor."

The captain replied, "No liquor." Then, from his pocket, the captain pulled out a pouch of cut tobacco, which he handed to the Indian. The additional gift pleased the chief, who, in return, offered a pony for sale. There being no takers, Ferguson and the chief continued their sign-language conversation, incomprehensible to the nearby emigrants. Finally, the chief offered the peace sign, remounted his pony, and rode off with the other mounted braves.

Wagon members rushed up to the captain, asking questions about the encounter: "What did they want?" "Are they friendly?" "Where are our soldiers?" "Can we go on?"

"Calm yourselves. Yes, they are friendly now but weren't when they first appeared. You could see they had no squaws or children with them but were dressed and armed for battle with lances, arrows, and rifles. It's not as if they just showed up asking for a prayer meeting with us. They are Oglala Sioux and wanted to force a trade from us . . . it was either trade or fight. As you noticed, I chose to trade. I consider it more like a payment or tribute for passing through their land. I gave them a blanket and a coil of thin copper wire, which they will use for themselves or trade with other tribes. They seemed pleased with the offering and gave us permission to ride through their territory but not to hunt.

"They asked if we carried the smallpox with us and if we had traded with other Indians and where. I told them we carried no smallpox. These being Sioux, with their own trading network, I knew they were concerned that we had traded with other Indians, interfering with or trading with their competition. I told them we had traded with no other Sioux, Cheyenne, or Crow. They seemed relieved and thankful. It is always a delicate situation negotiating with them."

One wagon master in the ranks yelled to Ferguson in a voice filled with sarcasm and loud enough for everyone to hear: "This is highway robbery. You let those dumb savages intimidate you by demanding these items for our passage on the trail? I thought it was the army that guaranteed our passage, not the savages. Furthermore, I thought they were paid by our government for this land, which they seem now to claim as their own."

"Yeah, yeah," echoed the assembled group of train members.

Ferguson looked directly at the angry man. "The chief offered me ten ponies for your wife. Should I have accepted the offer?" A few wagon bosses whispered to each other and smiled; the women stood shocked.

Ferguson continued, "Maybe you want to take on ten well-armed, well-mounted braves out here in the open. You go ahead, mister. But don't expect me to participate in your damned foolishness. There are easier ways to commit suicide. If you want a new captain, elect one." The crowd remained silent for a few moments, and then another question rose from the crowd.

"Where in hell is the army to kill these savages?"

"Sir, the army is spread thin all over the West trying to protect wagon trains, settlers, and the new telegraph and rail lines. They can't be everywhere at once."

"They sure as hell need to be on the Oregon Trail," another wagon master shouted to the captain.

"The simple fact is, we are all safe and have made our tribute payment to the Indians in return for safe passage," the captain replied, hoping to end the angry gathering.

Another voice spoke up. "I for one am pleased with the way our captain handled this situation. He should be complimented rather than criticized."

"You're right," another voice shouted, accompanied by some applause.

Then silence.

"All right now, let's hitch up and be ready to move on in ten minutes," the captain said in a commanding voice and then added, "I desperately need to get to Fort Laramie, where I have some important business to attend to."

Hearing no disagreement with the captain's order, the crowd broke up and returned to their wagons. But before they started out on the trail, two wagon masters, clearly bothered about something, approached Calvin.

The younger of the two, a scruffy character with sad, watery eyes and a serious frown, said in a soft voice, "The two of us want a new captain for this train. We're sick and tired of Ferguson's orders, his disregard for our comfort, lousy campsites, long hours on the trail, selection of guards, and no regard for those of us always sucking dust at the rear of the column. He acts like an autocrat, as if he were the biggest toad in the puddle; no one is allowed to question his orders. We're not the only angry folks in this train. Look at the way Ferguson made fun of that man and his wife in front of everyone. It was insulting and uncalled for. We want to call a meeting tonight and elect you as captain."

Calvin was shocked by the comments. He'd heard some grumbling along the trail from time to time but nothing that suggested a rebellion brewing within the ranks. He instantly responded, "Your comments are unwarranted. The captain served in the army and knows how to command a safe wagon train. Yes, he may appear autocratic in his manner, but if you'd ever served in the military, you'd appreciate his leadership qualities. He just recently negotiated us out of what could have been a very deadly situation. And given the number of wagon trains on the trail, it's not always easy to find the perfect overnight camp. Also, as you know, I post the guards, not the captain. I try to spread the guard duty responsibility evenly across the adult men. I'd suggest if you are so displeased with the leadership of this train and its progress that you drop out and join another train behind us or go it alone. It's your choice, but I'm not a candidate for a fool's errand."

The older of the two men said, "I'm leaving the train."

The younger one added, "I'm not trusting my life to Ferguson; I'm dropping out also."

The two men walked back to their wagons and pulled them out from the line.

Calvin reported the news to the captain. All he said was, "Good riddance to them. They're only troublemakers. I appreciate your advice to them, Calvin, and your loyalty to this train."

That afternoon, on the pretense of wanting some advice about fishing, Ferguson invited the attractive eighteen-year-old daughter of a widowed wagon master, Joseph Frolicker, to ride with him. The captain often asked a train member to join him on his wagon for company, but never a woman, and certainly not a beautiful young woman. Susanna Frolicker had gained some notoriety along the trail for her fishing skills. Her evening catch from the always nearby river earned her some money from other families unable to add variety to their evening meals.

Calvin heard from conversation with Susanna's father around the evening fire that the captain had plied the young woman with questions about where on the river to fish, what bait to use, the proper hook size, and the best length for a willow pole. He had also asked her more personal questions: her age, schooling, the location of their farm in the Ohio Valley, and their destination. Frolicker explained to Calvin that his wife had died in childbirth—a stillborn baby late last year—and that he wanted to put some distance between himself and their Ohio home, and start a new life with relatives near Sacramento, California. "I begged Susanna to stay behind in Ohio with her aunt and finish high school, but she wanted to be part of the adventure of moving west," Frolicker said.

Ferguson, sitting nearby earlier that afternoon, absorbed the answers while giving equal attention to Susanna's attractive appearance. Blond hair curled below her flowered bonnet, which framed her beautiful face highlighted by large blue eyes and a gorgeous smile.

Later that same evening, Calvin noticed that the captain had his eye on Susanna as she made her way to the river. She was bareheaded, wearing moccasins, and carrying her long willow fishing pole. Distracted by a burst of sparks from the fire, Calvin failed to notice the captain rush off to his wagon. Quickly, Ferguson washed, changed his shirt, and combed his dirty hair. He walked toward the river, where he found Susanna fishing. Before she knew what was happening, Ferguson grabbed Susanna from behind, pulled her to the ground, and began kissing her. She struggled unsuccessfully to break from his muscular embrace as the captain dragged her up the sandy bank into some brush. The rush of the river drowned out her screams. The captain ripped off Susanna's blouse, dropped his trousers to his knees, and ordered her to stop yelling; when she refused, he gagged her with part of her blouse. Ferguson growled at her to stop clawing at him as he tore off her pantaloons, spread her legs, and mounted her. Knowing her only choice was to succumb to his brutality, she lay helpless as he pressed, shoved, and thrust into her again, again, and again.

When Susanna did not show up at her wagon at dark, Mr. Frolicker went to the captain's wagon to report her absence. Not finding him there, Frolicker sought out Calvin at the evening fire. He pulled Calvin aside and reported his daughter missing. "She always returns from her evening fishing break for supper before dark . . . but not tonight," Frolicker said, his German accent more pronounced.

"I can't find the captain, so I've come to you for assistance. She may have had an accident. I need to search for her, but I have no horse. Can I use yours?" Frolicker pleaded, his eyes tearing up.

Hesitating as he remembered the captain eyeing Susanna earlier, Calvin said, "Let me go to the river. My horse is a bit rough mannered when it comes to a stranger on his back."

Calvin saddled the Morgan and immediately rode off to Ferguson's wagon. He noticed dirty clothing strewn about the usually neat interior and the dog chained to the side panel. He took a dirty shirt to the dog, let him smell it before he unchained him, and pushed him off the back of the wagon. "Go," he yelled. Calvin followed behind on horseback as the dog headed toward the river. Within seconds of reaching the water's edge, the dog looked to the top of the riverbank and ran in that direction. Calvin followed. There he found the captain on top of Susanna, humping away. When the captain saw his dog, he rolled off Susanna. Then he heard Calvin's angry command. **"GET TO YOUR FEET, NOW."** Breathing hard, with his pants tangled around his knees, the captain struggled to stand. In the process of getting to his feet, he bent over quickly and reached for his holstered pistol. Calvin pulled his own and fired. Ferguson's chest exploded with the first shot. With a second shot to the forehead, Ferguson fell back. His eyes rolled back into his skull, and a thin trickle of blood leaked from the corner of his mouth. Calvin leaped from his horse, rushed to Susanna's side, and ripped the gag from her mouth.

"Are you hurt?" Her bloodshot eyes stared into the distance; when she turned her head toward Calvin, she said nothing. Blood ran down the inside of her legs.

To allow her a moment of privacy to rearrange her clothing, Calvin directed his attention to the captain and dragged him away into some nearby brush. He turned to Susanna, who had secured her pantaloons and rearranged her torn blouse, and asked, "If I help you up into the saddle, do you think you can ride? I'll lead you back to camp." She nodded. Tears streaked the dirt on her fearful face. He carefully lifted Susanna up to the left stirrup, where she managed, with a boost, to swing herself onto the saddle and get her right foot into the opposite stirrup. As he led Barney back to camp, Susanna's eyes remained unfocused in a blank stare.

Calvin led her to the outside of the circle to avoid other wagon members. Leaving Susanna on his horse, he found Frolicker seated inside his wagon, reading a German Bible. He jumped up upon seeing Calvin enter.

"Did you find her?" he asked frantically.

"Yes," Calvin responded in an unusually frail voice.

"Then where is she?" Frolicker cried as he rushed to the wagon's opening.

Calvin grabbed Frolicker by the arm and forced him back onto the portable cot where his Bible lay open. He listened to the painful account Calvin gave him; no detail of the rape and the killing of Ferguson was spared. Calvin continued, "She is outside, transfixed in horror, unable to speak... be patient with her, and she will recover. I've seen the same mind-numbing shock in soldiers. They heal with time. Wait here and I'll bring her to you." Frolicker stood up to follow Calvin, all the while angrily muttering in German. Calvin pushed him back toward the cot and commanded firmly, **"Stay here."**

Calvin lifted Susanna gently from the saddle and brought her to the back of the Frolicker wagon. He and her father carried Susanna to the cot where she lay silent, staring up at the wagon's canvas top. Frolicker, fighting back tears, stroked her hair and whispered to her softly in German. Calvin left them together as he returned to his own wagon, where he unsaddled Barney, grained him, and asked Grace to join him outside.

"This evening I've had a horrible encounter. I found the captain violating a woman member of our train. It was a disgusting scene." Grace's eyes widened in shock, and then she asked, "Where?"

"Down by the river."

"Did you recognize the woman?"

"Yes, but we need to protect her identity. She's hurt and unable to speak. She's now under her father's care in their wagon."

"I bet it was that Frolicker girl, the one who rode with the captain this morning. He's had his eye on her since we left Council Bluffs."

Calvin nodded slowly, and then continued, "There's more to the story. I shot and killed the captain after he pulled a gun on me. He's lying dead close to the river and needs to be buried. I'll have to call a meeting of the wagon masters and report the killing and the incident that caused it."

"Can't you say he had an accident and leave it at that?"

"No, it's not the truth, and besides, if you saw his body, it sure doesn't look like an accident." Calvin wiped the sweat from his brow with the back of his hand as he sought a sympathetic look from Grace.

Calvin sent Hiram around to each wagon to announce an emergency meeting of the wagon masters. He could hear Hiram's voice as he related his message to the adjoining wagon. "There will be an emergency meeting in thirty minutes on the south side of the circle. Father says you must attend." Hiram rode off to inform the posted guards and then returned to rekindle the dinner fire.

Once all were assembled around the fire, Calvin stood facing the wagon masters and asked everyone to sit down. "I have some very serious news to announce. Earlier this evening, when one of our wagon mates failed to return from a trip to the river, I went on a search for her. I soon found her in the grasp of Ferguson, who was in the process of violating her. He had gagged her and pinned her to the ground on her back. When I ordered the captain to get to his feet, he reached for his pistol. Before he unholstered it, I shot him once in the chest and then again in the forehead. He was, I believe, dead before he hit the ground. His body is down near the river, where I plan to bury him this evening. I will report his death at the next army post, which will be Fort McPherson in two days. I assume I will be arrested, charged with murder, and brought before a territorial court. Because of these events, particularly the death of Ferguson and my involvement in the incident, I think it best I resign my position as deputy wagon captain. I have called this meeting for you to elect both a new captain and his assistant."

Only the small crackles from the fire broke the stunned silence.

Then a question from the back: "What about the girl? How's she doing?"

"She's hurt . . . not badly . . . needs to be with her family." Everyone could guess the name of the victim. They weren't fooled by Calvin's attempt to hide her identity.

Another man raised his hand. "Why must you report Ferguson's death? Who in hell will miss that son of a bitch?"

A voice shouted, "Yes, who?"

Calvin stood stunned by the suggestion. He knew the news of Ferguson's death would reach the authorities one way or another. *Better to be up front and honest,* he thought, *than hide the inevitable. The truth will eventually become known beyond the confines of the wagon train. If it comes to a trial, I believe Joseph Frolicker would volunteer to testify in my defense. But I must report it.*

"Ferguson may be missed by his family, though I'm not certain that he has one," Calvin responded.

A loud voice from one of the bachelor miners filled the momentary silence. "As far as I'm concerned, Ferguson died today of cholera. I'll rummage through his wagon and look for any correspondence. If I find anything, I'll hand it over to Mr. Marlow. If there is money in his belongings, and I imagine there is, it will be shared with all the wagons after we elect and compensate Calvin Marlow as our new captain." Shouts of "aye" filled the air, and then died down when Joseph Frolicker strode up to the fire.

He stopped, put his hand on Calvin's right shoulder, and announced to the assembled men, "I'm sorry to be late, but my daughter was viciously attacked this evening." He then went on to detail the attack and Calvin's role in rescuing his daughter. "Calvin, in the eyes of the Lord, you did the right thing. I sure would have done the same, and I doubt that there is a man here who wouldn't have pulled the trigger on Ferguson." The silence of the men around the fire confirmed Frolicker's statement.

A few men shifted uncomfortably, unwilling to look at Frolicker. After a long silence, the miner who had suggested Ferguson died of cholera announced, "Now let's hear some support for Calvin Marlow. He's helped us along the trail in all conditions, and he's demonstrated to us his common sense and courage. Who's in favor of electing Marlow as captain?" Shouts of "Marlow, Marlow," resounded through the air as women and children poked their heads out of their wagons in reaction to the commotion.

Calvin stood up, his eyes watering, and said, "I thank you for your support and confidence . . . but I cannot serve as your captain." He removed his hands from the pockets of his bloodstained pants and continued. "Most of you are headed for California. My family and I are headed to Colorado, which means we must leave the train in four days once we reach the South Platte."

Someone pleaded, "But at least continue on with us until we reach Fort Laramie in Wyoming."

"I won't say no, but I'll have to speak with my wife. And I think I know what she'll say."

Then Frolicker stood and announced, "OK now, let's put off this election until Calvin decides on his plans. What we need now are some volunteers to help dig a grave." Four men stood up to join Frolicker. They said they'd be back shortly with shovels and some extra canvas.

At the river, two men lifted the bloody corpse onto the canvas, wrapped it, and tied it securely with rope. After digging a hole, they lowered Ferguson slowly into the sandy earth. With tears flowing, Frolicker stood beside the grave and mumbled a few words in German. The men shoveled four feet of sand onto Ferguson. The group then walked off in silence.

Back at his wagon, Calvin slumped down onto the makeshift bed. Grace told the children to play outside near the fire, and then she came to her husband with a small glass of brandy and water, held his hand tight, and kissed him on his dirty forehead. "Thinking back about the captain," Grace said in a soft voice, "we really didn't need him on the trail. All we do every day is follow the grave markers. I won't miss his filthy language. Do we even need a new captain?"

"I don't know," Calvin answered. "At the meeting, the wagon masters asked me to be their captain. I told them we were headed to Colorado and would leave the train at the junction of the South Platte. Then one man asked if I wouldn't consent to stay with the train at least until Fort Laramie. That would probably mean a ten-day detour for us, but also some extra money. I said I'd like to talk with you before I made any final decision."

Grace collected her thoughts. "As you must know, Calvin, this voyage can't end soon enough for me. I know you and all the wagon masters think this journey west is a great adventure. But right now I'd trade that adventure for some good old-fashioned comfort. The children are ready to settle down. How many more wind- and sandstorms, which cut through us like a butter knife, must we endure? The oxen have lost weight. How much more can they take? And what about the Indians, who are reportedly more numerous and warlike on the Laramie Road than where we're headed? And if we're headed to California, I don't want to end up like the Donner Party. If it weren't for the damned snakes, I'd be happy to stay right here and carve out a farm." Then Grace added with a smirk, "And watch over Ferguson's grave."

"Seems like you've made up your mind."

"Yes, you could say that. I also believe I speak for the children. Hiram has already gone through the soles of the new boots we bought him in Vermont, and I don't think Cornelia has yet recovered from our boat trip on Lake Erie. As for me, if they can supply me with a new back at Fort Laramie, I say let's go on. But if not, I much prefer to take my chances in Julesburg than to endure ten more days of dust, rain, windstorms, and what we saw in the distance two days ago—a tornado. To be honest with you, Calvin, I've come to think fondly of Vermont and its rocks. The only rocks around here have to have been brought in by wagon."

As a precautionary measure, Calvin banned all morning and evening fires that night and the next day. A cold meal and no morning coffee led to numerous questions and complaints, to which he responded, "The smoke from the fires might signal to the Indians the presence of a wagon train. Troopers at Fort Kearny warned me that the country from here to the South Platte River is dangerous. We need to be on the lookout for some unfriendly Sioux."

The same morning the train headed out on schedule. One of the bachelors from the miners' wagon led Ferguson's oxen and wagon on foot right behind the Marlows'. When Calvin noticed that the miner had little experience leading oxen, he sent Hiram back to lend assistance and offer some gentle teenage advice to the novice teamster.

At the midmorning break, everyone noticed clouds of smoke rising in the west. Within a half hour, the smoke clouds had expanded to where a dusty haze engulfed the wagon train and the surrounding prairie. Calvin sent a scout ahead to investigate the cause of the smoke. The scout returned with news of a huge prairie fire.

"The plains are black as far as I could see to the west. In places, it has jumped across the river. With the wind, the fire is headed this way at a pretty good clip."

"See any Indians?" Calvin inquired.

"No, just burned grass, smoke, and some wildlife, including a herd of buffalo followed by a pack of wolves, running this way, away from the fire."

Calvin had the word passed along the line that the train would take cover down on the river, where the cottonwoods were too green to burn. His instructions also included this advice: "Keep your canvas wet and your water buckets full, and watch for flying sparks."

Calvin rode back along the wagon line with the acting scout to give directions. "Don't know what started it," they kept repeating in answer to the same question.

The fire moved at about five miles an hour and soon consumed the drier grasses surrounding the trail, but it failed to touch any of the wagons or livestock, which, in some cases, sought protection in the river. On shore, wagon members scampered about beating out sparks or carried water buckets to patches of small fires. Calvin walked around the scattered wagon train to inspect any damage. Only one canvas cover had suffered a large burn, and a patch of wheel grease had caught fire on another wagon, damaging a spoke. The smoke caused more discomfort than the fire itself.

Calvin didn't want to move the train at midday for fear they'd be camping that night in a burned area with no forage for livestock. He decided on an early departure the next day instead, and with a full day's travel, he hoped it might be possible to get beyond the burn and back into grass country close to Fort McPherson. The small garrison had a reputation as a well-placed resting spot.

As planned, Calvin had the wagon train assembled and on the move by first light. Those leading their oxen and most of the teamsters wore wet bandannas across their faces to protect against the black soot. At the midmorning rest, everyone headed for the Platte to wade into the cool water with soap to wash the soot from their faces, hands, and clothes. The warm air had dried their clothes by midday.

The train soon encountered a cavalry company from Fort McPherson headed east on the trail. Calvin asked the lieutenant in charge about Indians in the area. He said only a few remained. Most of them had been pushed north into Wyoming.

Calvin asked what he knew about Julesburg. "Heard it was attacked last year?"

"True, the original town got attacked by the Sioux last December," the lieutenant replied. "But the town is now rebuilding closer to the river, where it's more easily defended by Fort Sedgwick, which is being reinforced. There will be new shops, even a boardinghouse. It's a major intersection for emigrants headed west and is destined to grow with the new rail line coming through the town soon, headed to California."

"Farmers moving into the area?"

"Haven't seen too many, but there are herds of cattle, and even some woolies," the lieutenant replied.

"If Fort Sedgwick is being reinforced, why are you and your troops heading in the opposite direction?" Calvin asked.

"We're headed east for Fort Kearny, where we're to meet General Sherman and accompany him to Fort Sedgwick. He's on an inspection trip. He'll be stopping at McPherson on his way. I'm hoping Billy Boy will close that shithole and send us to some more comfortable post."

"How far before we leave this burn?" Calvin inquired.

"'Bout ten miles . . . just short of McPherson and the junction with the South Platte."

"Indians, I'm guessing?"

"It's either the Oglala Sioux, Cheyenne, or Arapaho, or maybe all three. They figure the fires will keep the settlers out of their territory. Safe travels to you and your train, sir. If you want to help rid this territory of Indians, kill their commissary . . . the buffalo. As Billy Boy says, 'A dead buffalo is five dead Indians.'"

The lieutenant ordered his troops forward, and they made their way around the wagons. Women and children waved and offered raisins to the soot-dusted soldiers. In return, the troopers tipped their caps in thanks.

The train moved through the burned grass while the wind carried intermittent sparks from the surrounding trees. By dusk, they'd reached Fort McPherson, with its dilapidated buildings and its small assemblage of sloppily dressed troops. The fort was home to three undermanned infantry companies and the skeleton of a cavalry company. The commanding officer, a captain, directed the wagon train to a clearing just north of the cottonwood barracks. Calvin glanced inside the half-hinged door and saw four soldiers in their skivvies gathered around a deck of cards and a bottle. Dirty uniforms lay on the dirt floor. He turned to the captain, who stood by the door in a frayed tunic, to say something from two feet away, but before he did, the strong smell of the liquor interrupted his thought. He wanted to tell the captain, "Put a lighted match close to your mouth, and you'll explode like an artillery shell."

Calvin dispensed with a circle and allowed evening and morning fires. After supper, he called for a meeting of the wagon masters. They knew without being told that the purpose of the gathering was to elect Marlow or someone else as wagon captain.

"I see everyone made it safely through the fires with little damage, and I appreciate everyone's assistance, particularly your cooperative spirit. I'm also pleased to see we all have the same taste in clothing . . . black," began Calvin. Everyone looked around and laughed. "At our last gathering, the evening of Ferguson's death, you all decided to delay the election of a new captain until we reached the point where the Denver Road along the South Platte takes off from the North Platte. Well, that junction is just ahead of us."

A man dusted in soot stood and asked Calvin if he would be staying with the train or leaving for Colorado.

Calvin replied that he'd talked with his family and it was their decision to stay with their original plan and head toward Julesburg.

"No, no!" came shouts from the gathering. Another man stood. "Calvin, I've talked with some of our wagon masters. They said that if you'll agree to serve as our captain from here to California, we'll pay you double the salary that we were going to pay Ferguson."

"I appreciate the offer, gentlemen, but I can't do it. My wife is hurting and needs some rest, and my children are exhausted. There are others here equally as capable as me. It's time to get on with your election. I'd like to nominate my assistant, Jake Cousins. He's an army veteran from the Ohio Valley, fought at Chancellorsville and Bull Run, and as a former sergeant he's a battle-tested leader."

A voice from the group called out, "I'll second that."

A long silence fell over the emigrants. Every wagon master knew Cousins and respected his judgment and quiet manner. Another wagon master stood up and declared, "Nominations closed." The vote was unanimous. Cheers went up for Cousins as men walked up to him and congratulated him. He immediately announced, "Tomorrow will be a layover day ... time for repairs and for women to do their laundry." More cheers filled the air.

That same evening, Calvin visited the post commander's quarters, a log cabin with roof shingles and a glass window missing, the latter replaced by a dirty piece of canvas. He knocked on the plank door. "Enter," came the response. The captain looked up from the table where a document and a half-empty bottle of bourbon kept him company.

"What you want, mister?"

"Sir, I need to make a report of a murder that occurred on the trail before we arrived here."

"An Injun, I hope." The captain helped himself to a couple of ounces of bourbon from the bottle. "Have a snort?"

"Just a sip, thanks." The captain poured out an ounce into a dirty cup.

"No, sir, not an Indian but our wagon train captain, a former army sergeant."

"So why tell me about this killing? What do you want me to do, find the killer and hang him?" the captain asked, his words slurred.

"No, sir. I need to confess to the murder of our captain, and not knowing of any courts in this territory, I thought it best to report the killing to the military authorities."

"Mister, you need to know that in this territory we have whites killing whites, whites killing niggers, and Indians killing Indians every week. But when Indians kill a white, that's the only news that catches my attention. And right now I got me plenty of problems with these here redskins . . . a shortage of ammo and horses to fight 'em . . . plus deserters . . . three left just this week. I ask for replacements, and the army sends me eleven niggers who ain't seen a horse before and a fourteen-year-old Irish boy bugler. I don't need no more fucking problems, especially from a civilian like you."

"Others in our wagon train know about the killing, and they'll probably report it, sir." Calvin went on to detail the killing and the events surrounding it.

"Sure sounds to me like you had good cause to kill the son of a bitch. If you're so intent on reporting the killing, report it to the civil authorities. But you won't find any around this territory. I've been commander here coming on two years, and I ain't never seen no sheriff or law enforcement official. If you're looking to get yourself arrested, I'd get yourself back to Omaha or maybe down Julesburg way . . . but Julesburg is in Colorado Territory, where I can assure you they won't give a rat's ass about what you did in Nebraska. But if you're really hankering to get yourself arrested and face a judge, I'd keep on down the road to Denver City. You homesteaders sure have outpaced the law.

"As for me, I don't have no connection with them civil authorities. I answer only to my commander, General Billy Boy Sherman, and not very often at that. If you think the army or the civil courts give a coot about your killin', you're fooling yourself. There's killins going on all the time . . . can't be investigatin' every one of them. And as I said, I have bigger things to worry about . . . like killin' Indians. Since you buried the body somewhere on the trail, my advice to you, sir, is to forget the whole thing. Just keep goin' on down the road and get on with your business. Why stir up trouble for me and yourself when it can be avoided?"

Calvin thanked the captain for his "profound advice," emptied his cup, and walked back to his wagon.

Grace had spent the layover day with the children, washing and mending clothes in the morning and reading to them in the afternoon. The children always gave their full attention to this special ritual. Grace would mimic the speech of the characters and enhance the story with the pace and rhythm of her reading. When she ended, the thrilled audience shouted, "More, more!"

Later that afternoon, in the fading sunlight before supper, she wrote to her brother.

Summer, 1866
Dear Jonathan,

Here we are at Fort McPherson and hardly a sober soldier to be seen. This place, and the soldiers who man it, are a discredit to both the army and the nation. I suspect that more than half are immigrants, mostly Irish and Germans.

For two days we've traveled through a burned area, the fire set by the Indians, according to an army lieutenant, to keep all wagon trains from passing through their country. But last night, Calvin talked with a sergeant who said he and four other soldiers at Fort McPherson had set the fire, not the Indians. The sergeant said that his commanding officer ordered him to burn the plains to keep the buffalo and the Indians out of the country. Apparently, the fort commander believed he could not defend the fort against an Indian attack with the few troops he had at hand and after the Sioux made off with half their horses.

After some terrible problems with our wagon captain, the wagon masters pleaded with Calvin to stay with them as their replacement leader 'til California. They offered him a very generous salary. But again, we'll stay with our original plan and take the Denver Road to Julesburg. We want to get settled as soon as possible. I don't know what to expect in Julesburg. We've received reports of Indian attacks in and around the town last year, including a fire that destroyed almost all of Julesburg. But the army tells us that Julesburg has rebuilt itself in the shadow of a strengthened Fort Sedgwick, and that the town is now the center of trade for those headed southwest two hundred miles toward Denver City or northwest to Montana on the Bozeman Trail. The freighters call it the "Overland City." The army assures us of the excellent agricultural opportunities in the area. Personally, I'm not one to accept on faith any assurances from our army, though Calvin, like most veterans, rarely questions either their effectiveness or their veracity.

Calvin and the other men in our train all seem to consider this journey to the West "a great adventure," a way for them to prove to themselves and others their manly skills. I thought the Civil War was proof enough. For me and probably other women on the trail, we have nothing to prove, except maybe that we are equal to the men, if not superior, in protecting our children from accidents, disease, starvation, and the elements. Who serves as the camp cooks each evening? Women. I fail to see this as a great adventure. I'd much prefer to trade a little adventure for some good old-fashioned comfort.

I can't wait for this trip to end. I tire of bumping along in the wagon, the constant wind in our faces from the west. I don't want to see more notes pinned to trees like the one I saw this morning. "For Ike Swann. We buried your brother a mile back on the trail after he died of cholera. The grave site, just off the trail to the north, can be identified by a cross made from willows." I've seen too many graves, Jonathan, of emigrants who have died of cholera, dysentery, tetanus, mountain fever, snakebite, brain congestion, laudanum overdose, suicide, or murder. What warnings can be delivered by the dead?

Please write us at the Julesburg post office and tell me of activities at home. I do miss it and hearing about family.

With all my love,
Grace

After supper on the day of arrival, Grace had put the children to bed and Calvin returned to the wagon. Grace asked, "Where have you been?"

"Visiting with the captain again," Calvin replied and then suggested to Grace that they sit outside.

They sat on the wagon tongue. Grace said with some annoyance that she knew Calvin had been with the captain, judging from his breath.

"Yes, we had a drink and talked again about Ferguson and the killing. He really doesn't want to act on my report. 'Get yourself down the road and forget about it.' That was his advice."

"Sounds like good advice to me," Grace replied. "Now come to bed."

They fell asleep in each other's arms.

July 1866; Julesburg, Colorado Territory

Everyone was happy to be leaving Fort McPherson with its motley troops and useless commander. Still, the insufferable heat played on their nerves. At the midmorning water break, six wagon masters approached Calvin and asked if he had reconsidered going to Colorado. Two women tried to weaken his resolve with a fresh fruit pie, baked the night before at the fort. His answer, however, remained the same.

That evening the train made camp at the confluence of the South and North Platte Rivers, where a colony of Germans had settled in a small community they named North Platte. Sandbars and small islands covered with willows hid the colony, which greeted the wagon train. One wagon master figured they'd traveled close to three hundred miles from their departure point in Iowa and 110 miles from Fort Kearny.

Some wagons had reached a critical juncture on the trail. Did they want to continue toward Oregon and California or end their trip more quickly in Colorado? Two wagons originally headed for California opted for Colorado and attached themselves to the Marlows' Colorado-bound train. It numbered seven wagons, headed down the South Platte Road so that they wouldn't have to make a river crossing. The Oregon-and-California-bound train, however, could not avoid a crossing of the South Platte to get to the North Platte Road headed west. Everyone recognized the dangers of the soft river bottom and its quicksand, which could suck humans, livestock, and wagons underwater and return only air bubbles to the surface. Calvin led the entire train to what the *Prairie Traveler* called California Crossing, three miles west of Julesburg, and reportedly "a safe, shallow section of the river in August, with a firm bottom."

One wagon master volunteered to test the crossing. Calvin tied him to a rope and, with three other wagon masters on shore, held him tight. The volunteer walked gingerly through the shallow river, all the while feeling the river bottom with his bare feet and looking down into the semi-clear water. Suddenly, he sank in the sand up to his knees and, seconds later, to his waist. The four at the end of the rope yanked on the lifeline and pulled their companion free from the soft sand. Once on shore, the volunteer sandhog searched for another potential crossing. He waded out into the river, this time moving faster, and reached the far shore without much difficulty. Everyone cheered his success. He crossed back on the same path, informing those on shore, "The trick is to keep moving . . . and as fast as possible. There is just enough water in the riverbed to lubricate the quicksand. If you stop in that stream, the sand takes over. I'd suggest that every wagon be double-teamed. Once across, any team with a stout rope can be used as an additional tugger in the event a crossing wagon bogs down. It is critical to keep those oxen moving. Whip the shit out of 'em if you have to."

A younger wagon master stepped forward and volunteered his stout team to be the first to cross the South Platte and act as the onshore tugger. Another wagon volunteered to double-team on the first crossing. The wagons lined up as Calvin guided each to the precise crossing point. He warned the wagon of bachelor miners, "Don't you be stopping midstream to fish. Nothing in there but hungry sharks." They looked at him in horror. The driver of their wagon started whipping his oxen long before their feet touched the shallow stream, and once in the water, one miner manned a whip while the other miner with a makeshift willow spear, kept a sharp eye out for sharks. Other wagons lined up and prepared for the crossing. With every wagon safely across the river, the wagon masters all thanked Calvin for his leadership on the trail with a "Hip, hip, hurray!" One woman wept as she waved with one hand, blew a kiss with the other, and shouted, "We'll miss you, Calvin and Grace."

The Marlows and the six other wagons headed southwest, following the South Platte's sandy riverbed toward Julesburg. To the west, the bed flattened out to accommodate spring run-off from the Rockies and narrowed where the landscape took a dip toward the east. The sound of the wagons scared off some ducks and geese and an occasional heron from the river. Grace gazed at the only two trees in sight.

"God sure skimped when He planted trees out here." Her wry remark only began to suggest her disappointment if not anger.

"Surely when we get to Julesburg we'll see trees and building materials," Calvin tried to reassure her. "God sure wrung all the moisture out of the air. But look at that grass. Got to be good soil underneath to grow it. Sure is nothing like that back in Vermont."

Grace tried to show her enthusiasm for the country. "The air does taste better here. Maybe that's why the birds sing louder." Then she pointed toward the sky. "And look at that rising quarter moon behind that lead-colored cloud."

As they moved on toward Julesburg, they passed two ranches on the well-traveled road. The occupants made their living not by farming but by caring for a few animals and serving as way stations along the trail. They sold meals and an assortment of goods—grain and hay for livestock, gunpowder, saddles, tobacco, ax handles, matches, and liquor of unknown origin or content. Wagon trains often overnighted at these ranches, where emigrants like the Marlows sought shelter during a severe storm or made critical repairs to wagons.

On the east side of the tiny town of Julesburg, the Marlows approached a large collection of tents and wagons, the inhabitants of which were either emigrant pioneers like the Marlows, in search of new agricultural opportunities, or miners headed for the diggings. The thirty-wagon encampment was the size of a small town. Some cattle grazed near the riverbed. Three dogs fought over a large bison bone while two men helped a companion replace a shoe on a large, ill-tempered Shire stud. Children scampered around in search of buffalo chips. At supper that evening, Calvin introduced himself and his family to others at the camp while a fiddle played a jig in the background and everyone swatted flies. He was surprised to learn that all the wagon masters he encountered at the encampment had come out of the Midwest and West—Michigan, Iowa, Wisconsin, Ohio, and Kansas.

"Why no grain fields around here?" Calvin asked one of the wagon masters.

"Mister, all that grassland you see in the distance looks so flat and welcoming. But if you get up close and into the middle of it, you'll discover it's not all even and flat. It is filled with big holes and buffalo wallows, and if you try and put a plow into the grass, it's got deep, tough roots searching for some moisture in this dry land. If you plan to plow, you'll need to find yourself a friendly banker who'll lend you a small fortune to pay for all the shares you'll have to replace. Go out west beyond town about three miles and give a gander at the single acre some damned fool tried to turn last month. You'll see a broken plowshare for

THE GO-BACKER

every furrow he cut. Even if you could get a plow into this turf and plant some seed, I learned from folks already settled here that there's so little rain even the grasshoppers died of thirst during the droughts of sixty-four and sixty-five. Some damned fool from back east claimed that rain always follows the plow. That coot needs to haul his fat ass out here and find us some rain. But one thing you can say for this buffalo grass, cattle fatten on it and it carries nourishment throughout the winter, unlike most prairie grasses."

"I'm surprised so many families are here in this encampment rather than on a homestead claim."

"No land office here or even close to here. Land ain't been surveyed yet ... probably another year before it is ... then we'll file on a homestead. In the meantime, I'm lookin' for a place to squat."

Calvin lay awake thinking about how he'd been misled about the "agricultural opportunities" in Colorado. *Why didn't the newspapers, official reports, or travel books mention the need for surveys before homesteads became available? No one mentioned anything about the lack of rain or the deep sod. Julesburg may be the perfect strategic crossroads to and from Denver City and the trails west to Montana and California, but if I can't plow the ground and farm it, we'd be better off back in Vermont. All I see are cattle, some sheep, and horses. I'm not a stockman but a grain farmer; besides, I don't have the cash to buy cattle, and if I did, where would I graze them? On government land? Should we move on, go back, or stay? What does a farmer from back east know about the prairie grasses that surround me except maybe as feed for livestock? This western landscape is alien to me.*

I can see no clear end to the prairie in front of me. It just seems to evaporate where the green grass meets the blue sky. There are no identifying markers on the horizon, not a cabin, a tree, or a bluff. No, not even a sand dune, just a boring ocean of grass as far as the eye can see. It may be, as Grace says, pretty, but what use is pretty? You can't eat it.

I'd imagined rows of grain in manageable-sized plots that could be plowed in a week, planted in another week, and followed by ample summer rains to water the plants until fall harvesttime. Even in a dry Vermont summer, we'd have a small crop from which we could derive some income. But rain did not follow my rusty plow. I had no conception of an endless landscape teeming with livestock whose movement is controlled not by fences or picket lines but by the force of wind and the location of water. If we remain in this country, we'll have to learn how to best use this land rather than how to challenge it.

The next day, Hiram on Barney and Calvin driving the wagon rode into Julesburg to investigate the town and, after that, to inspect the small patch of plowed prairie on the far side of town. On first sight, seeing all the tents and shacks scattered around the main street, Calvin couldn't believe the town hadn't blown away in the winds they'd experienced on the trail. The one brick building housed the telegraph office, post office, and the stage station. A billiard parlor/saloon occupied the town's only frame building where, Calvin quickly learned, the rail workers made their second home along with every hustler, huckster, and gambler in the territory. The three other small structures, all adobe, along the town's single street housed a blacksmith shop, a vacant dry goods store, and a bakery with a FOR SALE sign in its broken window. Between two stores, a well-used trail headed north to a stable, where the Pony Express maintained an office and a corral for its remounts. A sign nailed to the corral directed the traveler to Fort Sedgwick.

Father and son rode out toward the farm with the patch of plowed ground. Calvin stood inspecting a sun-hammered row of green sod with its baked underbelly of dried roots exposed. *Yes,* Calvin thought, *four inches would be a challenge for my* plow. And even if successful, I don't own a heavy harrow with which to break up the thick sod."

As Calvin stood inspecting the furrows, a man appeared in the distance at the top of the field next to an adobe structure. Calvin assumed the man to be the owner—middle-aged, hunched over, and dressed in tan canvas pants, a patched cotton shirt with its sleeves torn off at the shoulders, well-worn work boots, and a sweat-stained straw hat.

He walked up to the Marlows and in a flat, unfriendly voice asked, "You lookin' for someone?"

"Yes, I'm new to this country, and my son and I were riding around looking at various lands. I was interested to see that someone had plowed a few acres of this prairie."

"That someone is me . . . Zack Brewster from Marion, Ohio, and a damned fool I am for comin' out here and puttin' a plow into this here damned sod. Let me tell you, God never intended for this prairie to be plowed."

Calvin noticed Brewster to be a shade deaf as he introduced himself and Hiram. "We're from Vermont, where I'm accustomed to cultivating five acres in a day. Never seen sod this thick with such a tangle of roots. Tough plowin', is it?"

"You're goddamned right it is. Broke two good plows in that little patch . . . first a busted brace and then a bent share. The town's blacksmith couldn't strengthen the share properly, and then when I ruined another share, I said no more plowin' for me. I only did it because I intended to file on this quarter section for a homestead . . . I needs to show some cultivation to prove up on it. If a John Deere can't cut into the deep sod, there ain't nothing can, 'cept maybe more horsepower and a stouter plow. You're lookin' to plow, mister?"

"Brought with me a Deere and some grain," Calvin responded. "Heard back east this was good farming country for grains, like wheat or maybe some corn."

"Bunch of balderdash, that's what they told you," Zack Brewster replied and then spit some tobacco juice into the dry soil. "Sure good soil for grain . . . a sandy loam and no rocks . . . but it's sure hell gettin' to it." He hesitated a moment, then looked directly at Calvin. "Where you settled?"

"Haven't yet. I'd planned to file on a homestead, but I found out just yesterday this country has no land office where I can file and won't until it's surveyed."

"That's the sum of it, mister, and probably won't be surveyed 'til next year or maybe later. Those of us who've settled here are what them government folks call 'squatters.' If you squat on a piece of ground before the land is surveyed, you get first right to make it your homestead claim. They call it 'preemption,' whatever the hell that means. You gotta show the government you've made some improvements . . . that's what I'm livin' in now, the claim shack. But I've squatted here long enough. Can't be waitin' no longer . . . can't plow no more, run out of patience but mostly money, plus a bad back from workin' with them wild horses around here. It's tough work trappin' 'em and then breakin' 'em for sale. Every one of 'em got a bad attitude, believe me. I'm a wantin' to head back to Ohio for an easier life.

"If you're looking for a place to settle, this land and shack can be yours. I'm needin' some coin to get me back home. For a small fee, I'll sell you this place . . . Live here in this claim shanty, plus this one hundred and sixty acres will be yours after the survey, the improvements already in place. What you say?"

"I'm not a cattleman . . . just a grain farmer. Besides, I'm not sure my family or I want to live out here on the prairie with Indians roaming the area."

"Mister, dem Indians are long gone. Army pushed them north into Wyoming and the Dakota Territories. Haven't seen no redskins around these parts in over a year. You got neighbors upriver and downriver. And dem soldiers at Fort Sedgwick

THE GO-BACKER

just downriver keep these parts safe from the redskins. Believe me, there's no better grass than right here. Blue grama, needlegrass, bluestem . . . you name it, we got it. Buy yourself a small herd, and in no time, you'll double your investment. I've seen it happen with a couple of homesteaders upriver. And with the railroad a comin', you'll have access to eastern markets. If I had me some cash and a better back, that's what I'd be doin.'"

"What's this I hear about claim jumpers coming in here and taking over a claim?" Calvin asked. "I'm not certain I want that kind of trouble."

"Nothin' much to worry about. We have ourselves a Homestead Claim Protective Association for this entire area around Julesburg. They act like a local land office, but with guns. They keep the books on who claimed what land and when, including the specific locations and boundaries. Anyone who comes in after you and wants to squat on your land and lay a claim will be told by the protective society to move along. If they don't move, they're forced to up and go . . . usually at gunpoint. They buried two jumpers just last month. If I sell to you, you pick up my date of settlement on this quarter section, with sod piles to mark the corners, and the protection of the association."

"What you askin' for your place?"

"Hundred in coin, or hundred and forty in greenbacks, will buy you the land, my home, most of the furnishings, 'cept for the cookstove, and all the improvements . . . it can be yours in two days. Lands for sale around these parts by dem land speculators are sellin' for more, without improvements and with a good hike to the river."

"I'd like to see what you're livin' in."

The farmer walked with Calvin and Hiram up a path to the sixteen-by-twenty-foot adobe structure. Outside, Calvin gave a quick glance at the farmer's two-horse team, whose size, confirmation, and condition failed to impress him. *It's no wonder the Ohio man's small team couldn't plow the sod,* he thought. Inside the structure, a gaunt woman in a ragged, faded blue homespun dress looked up, expressionless, from a washtub and gave him an unfriendly nod.

"It's not much, but it's served us well," Brewster said as he pointed with pride to the adobe brick walls, but without mentioning the small portion of the sod roof that had collapsed in the southwest corner. The dirt floor, hardened with buffalo tallow, was covered with two longhorn hides; a small sink on a stand stood next to a water barrel; and a rusted cookstove occupied the wall opposite a bed and two stacked wood cartons stuffed with clothing. A small, scarred pine table with a candle affixed in the middle and two wooden barrels for seating occupied the cabin's center space.

The farmer volunteered, "Get our water from a six-foot well just down the lane toward the river. In the later summer, when the river has an alkali taste, our well is one hundred percent good-tasting water. Everyone loves it, particularly the livestock. Army troopers sometimes come all the way over from the fort to water their horses here."

Hiram looked up at Calvin when he responded to the farmer with some hesitation. "A bit pricey . . . but let me think about it. I'll be back in a day or so after talking with my wife."

The Marlows walked back to the wagon, both looking intensely at the grass. As they started to ride upriver to further inspect the prairie, Hiram shouted to his father, "Look, look," as he pointed excitedly at three buffalo close to the river on the opposite side.

"Big bulls in good flesh," Calvin said. "Look carefully, just beyond the buffalo, and you'll see a pack of wolves. They're no threat to the buffalo unless they find an injured one . . . probably hunting up a jackrabbit or two. Off to the right over there are some antelope. There's probably a water hole with a spring where they've gathered."

They continued on the barren, well-traveled road, on the lookout for cattle. A small herd of young steers accompanied by a single cowboy appeared on the north side of the river. They selected a shallow crossing and, without trouble, crossed quickly, then headed through the grass and sage to the cowboy, who turned and rode toward the unfamiliar wagon.

"Lookin' for lost cattle?" he asked father and son.

"No, just riding around looking at the country."

"Nice grass. You won't find any better . . . Nutritious, even in the winter," the cowboy volunteered with a big smile.

"Good cattle country! I can see that," Calvin replied as he looked off to the north and south. "Your land?"

"I wish. Most of it belongs to Mr. Iliff."

"Should I know him?"

"You should know the name. He's the biggest cattleman in these parts . . . controls most of the land 'tween here and Denver City, and from there all the way up to Cheyenne. What land he don't own belongs to the government, but he uses it anyway so he can control the water. Ain't no government people around to stop him."

"And the cattle?"

"Most all of dem is Mr. Iliff's. Now that the army has about cleaned out the buffalo and the Injuns, it's men like Mr. Iliff who pretty much control the grass around here. Mr. Iliff used to get his cattle from Texas until this year, when the Colorado territorial legislature banned Texas cattle in these parts because of the fever. He'd buy five thousand longhorn yearling steers and heifers from Charles Goodnight in Texas, another cattle baron. We'd trail 'em up here in the spring, summer 'em on this grass, and sell 'em in the fall in either Denver City or Omaha for a mighty big profit, I'm sure. He also sells cattle to feed the rail workers, the reservation Indians, and the army troops.

Now we keep our heifer calves and grow our herd from within, without the worry of Texas ticks and fever. Problem is, we now have to ride with them heifers throughout the winter . . . damned cold it is, shootin' wolves and coyotes, and breakin' ice on the river for some open water holes. This here package of heifers I'm movin' west to put together with some other yearlings and bulls. They need to get with them bulls soon, or they'll be late calvin' next spring. Altogether, I hear we got twenty thousand head. That's a lot of beef to keep track of, especially with them red-skinned bandits hangin' around."

"Good-looking heifers," Calvin told him.

"Sure are. And you should see them Shorthorn bulls. Mr. Iliff buys 'em in Illinois and ships 'em to Omaha. We trail 'em from there. They sure throw off some good-lookin' calves. Wish I had the money to buy some. Them yearlings, they'll put on at least two hundred pounds this summer. Come fall, we'll cut out the cattle of the squatters, those cattle Mr. Iliff lets run with his in return for grazing rights on their land and access to the river. Most of the Iliff heifers, as I said, will be held back into the herd; we'll sell all the steers, which we trail to the nearest rail line. If I see any critter with the fever, I'll kill it and leave it for the wolves and coyotes."

"Most of this land around here, it belongs to Mr. Iliff?"

"Just about all of it, 'cept maybe what dem redskins claim. We still run on it anyway. We've had our share of problems with the Injuns . . . lost a good number of cattle to them . . . Army helped us out most of the time by clearing out the buffalo and dem redskins."

"If a squatter wanted to use his own land, how would he keep Mr. Iliff's cattle off?"

"That's what them fences are for. Around here, the custom is you fence your land to keep cattle out. Makes it real hard for them poor squatters to be buildin' a mile of fence around a quarter section, especially with no logs around these parts. Know what I mean?"

"Sounds to me like Mr. Iliff has it all figured out."

"That's for sure," the cowboy responded. "There are some other big outfits forty miles upriver and down on the Arkansas, but we keep our cattle separate. Mr. Iliff, he do some tradin' with 'em like with Mr. Prowers upriver of us . . . but just to be neighborly."

"I may want to take over a quarter section around here. How many cattle would Mr. Iliff let me run with his?"

"Would depend on the water. If you're near or on water, he'd probably allow fifteen to twenty young yearlings; if they're older, probably no more than fifteen, or if they're pairs, maybe ten or more; dry cows, I'd guess about the same, but I ain't seen no squatter dry cows runnin' with us."

"Where might I make arrangements with Mr. Iliff?"

"He's got a rep in Julesburg. Works out of the telegraph office . . . name is Jeffries. He'll tell you how many, and he'll ask what your brand is. Easy man to work with, especially if you're near water; that's what I hear anyway."

"Thanks for the information. I may be contacting Mr. Jeffries." Hiram and Calvin shook the cowboy's hand before they rode off toward the encampment east of Julesburg. They scared up a covey of prairie chickens, which Calvin diminished by one with his shotgun. "Best meal on the prairie," he said to his son. "Now you try your hand with the gun," Calvin said, handing over the weapon to Hiram. Within minutes they came upon another covey. Hiram quickly raised the double-barreled shotgun and fired off one shot, missing the flying targets. "You need to squeeze the trigger, not pull it. When you pull it, you'll always pull it off the target to the right and below it. That's why you want to squeeze it with your eye always on the target." Hiram nodded that he understood the instruction.

Once back on the road, they passed the farmer's plowed plot and stopped to give it one more look. For over a minute, Calvin studied it again and then snapped the whip at the oxen to move on.

On the return trip, they stopped at the post office in Julesburg and picked up a letter from Grace's brother, Jonathan, and then made a visit to the blacksmith shop, where Calvin picked up two horseshoes.

"Nice shop you have here. Been here long?"

"About a year now. Got me some new business right now with the railroad line near here, plus the usual business from the fort. Them railroad boys is always breakin' something and needing it fixed by dinnertime, but they always pay . . . and in real cash. I'll be movin' to the north side of the river with the rest of the town . . . maybe in about a month."

"I understand that the town has already moved once from two miles west. Now it's got to move again? Why?"

"It moved over almost two years ago after the Indians attacked the town, emptied the warehouses of grain and weapons, then burned everything and killed fifteen soldiers out at Fort Sedgwick. We're moving again, this time over to the river's north side, so we'll be adjacent to the new rail line, the Union Pacific, coming through from Omaha and connecting us to somewhere out on the West Coast."

"That's a lot of moving around," Calvin said.

"Sure as hell is. But for business, I'll have to move with the town. Right now, I got no place to go to and can't afford to build . . . I'll just stay put until somethin' shows up in the new location. May buy something from the railroad once they put some of their land up for sale."

"The railroad has land to sell?"

"Sure do. Government gave them alternate sections along their rail line to help 'em with construction costs. They'll be selling it as soon as they get it surveyed . . . I hear real soon. The rail crew here tells me they need the money. I asked the rail manager in town what they'd be asking for the land. He told me the parcels close to town would be the most expensive, like five dollars an acre, farther out maybe as cheap as a dollar an acre, depending on how close they are to the railroad and the river. I'm not sure the manager knew for certain.

"There is certainly a demand for land. Folks movin' in here all the time, and I'm anticipating the railroad bringing more settlers. We're just a stop on the trail with only seventy residents but growin' every day from a sleepy stage station to a real town. The land agents are already settled in here to help easterners find a homestead . . . for a fee, of course. Hell, we got almost as many soft-handed land agents hereabouts as we got callused farmers. I don't know what all them farmers are lookin' for . . . good farmland, I suppose. Not much of it around here as far as I can tell."

The blacksmith continued, "The boosters say we're perfectly located as a trade center. But we ain't got much to sell, except what we trade from them redskins. The sportin' houses probably do the best trade, what with all them soldiers out at the fort and them rail workers swarming through town. But that's about it."

The blacksmith took an angle iron out of the fire. "All we got here is mostly a collection of patched tents, 'dobe huts, and dilapidated shacks filled with poor dreamers trying to hold on and find a better life. But I sure wish we had some damn peace and quiet in town rather than all the shootings and thievery going on. No one respects the law, and what there is of it, no one wants it enforced. Livestock are safer here than people. We probably have the largest cemetery for so small a town in the country. Our reputation as a place for hell-raisin' sure has spread, attractin' gamblers, outlaws, and thieves every day. Hell, we even have some old-time trappers livin' here. They're a nasty bunch, corned most of the time and quick with the trigger . . . plus, they're always askin' for credit.

"Some Methodist church back east sent an unwelcome missionary in here . . . rode all the way from Davenport, Iowa, he said, to bring some Christianity to this place. He sure as hell got his work cut out for himself. But given the number of ruffians already here, I suspect he'll last about as long as an unclaimed quart of whiskey placed on the main street."

"I haven't seen any evidence of the law around here," Calvin said. "No courts, sheriffs, or other lawmen?"

"Not a one. Too damned dangerous for the lawmen. Everyone walks around here armed. Even the women in town carry derringers. A sheriff with a badge would be a walking target. 'Bout the only law around here is the Homestead Claim Protective Association. You cross them boys, and you got yourself a pack of trouble. They've half filled our cemetery with claim jumpers."

In one sense, the lack of lawmen in the Julesburg area gave comfort to Calvin, who feared he might be a target of the law for the murder of the wagon captain back in Nebraska. *Maybe the law won't be following me into Colorado Territory, like the captain said back at Fort McPherson. If I buy that land upriver from town, I sure would like the presence of that protective association.*

"Good to be talking with you," Calvin said to the blacksmith as he paid for the two horseshoes and returned to the wagon with Hiram.

"Where you been all this time?" Grace asked with some annoyance as they pulled up to the temporary camp.

"Lookin' over the country," Calvin replied. Grace dropped her knitting.

"Seen any trees?"

"Couple near town. Probably all spoken for, however."

"Calvin, what are we going to do? This is cattle country, it's not grain country . . . everyone says that, right? And where are we going to live? I didn't come all this way bouncing from Vermont with my children to be living under a dirty half-tent with little to eat except antelope, prairie onions, and some bitter wild berries."

THE GO-BACKER

Calvin tried his best to calm Grace as Cornelia clutched her mother's tattered dress. He proceeded to outline their options.

"We can stay put somewhere near here as squatters and wait for the area to be surveyed, and then file for a homestead. Or we could buy surveyed land from the railroad. Or maybe we pay a squatter on the other side of Julesburg for his small adobe-sod home and try our hand at stock raising, primarily cattle. If Julesburg doesn't suit you, we could move on west to search for better farming land. And of course, we could pack up and go back home. That's the way I see it."

"The children and I are too exhausted to be moving again somewhere far off from here. Look at Hiram, the poor boy is a walking skeleton, and Sam looks like a starving bird. Maybe we should stay around here and make the best of it. We have few choices as I see it. There's no place for us back in Vermont anymore, and if we moved on west, the land could be worse than here, plus there may be more unfriendly Indians. I say we stay. We've some money to help us get settled, right?"

Calvin had to agree with Grace. "I must admit to some disappointment, given all the hoopla we heard about this area for farming. But still, it's a busy place for trade. People are coming and going all the time and looking for supplies, particularly food. I'm tired of the trail life, like you and the children. And people in town tell me there's a good living to be made around here with cattle."

They talked about the homestead and adobe-sod house, its furnishings, and its location on the river. "Some good game nearby," Calvin added, news he hoped might lift Grace's spirits.

The next morning, Calvin rode Barney through Julesburg and out west of town to visit with Brewster. The same three buffalo had moved to the river, where they watered. Birds pecked away on the buffalos' backs, feeding on lice. Calvin rode up the path past the settler's water well and tank to the adobe structure, where the owner greeted him.

"I see you're back," Brewster said. "Didn't bring no diseases with you, I hope," he added as he took Calvin's hand in his firm grip. "You bring me an offer?"

"Yes, and a good one," Calvin replied. They talked about the hot weather and the likelihood of rain. Then Brewster broke off the casual conversation.

"So what's your offer?"

"I'll give you seventy in coin or one hundred and ten in script . . . move in the end of the week."

"I'd sure prefer the one hundred and ten in coin," Brewster responded.

"Can't do it," Calvin answered. "But I will help you pack and load your wagon."

After a long silence, Brewster answered, "Looks to me like we got ourselves a deal." They shook hands, and Brewster handed Calvin the bill of sale to sign. "Don't lose this. You need to show it to the protective association in Julesburg."

Calvin read the short document describing the land, its location, and the sale price, and handed it back to Brewster, who signed it with his inked goose quill. The "Zack" was clear enough, but the "Brewster" looked more like a collection of prairie dog footprints.

"See you in two days," Calvin said as he mounted his horse. "In the meantime, look after that prairie marble on your roof," Calvin added, referring to a sagging sod patch.

"Sure will," Brewster responded as he waved back, smiling.

That evening, Calvin trimmed and reshod Barney's two front feet after watering and washing him at the river. He noticed with pleasure how the stud horse had kept his flesh and added some muscle to his rear, Barney's drive train. *He'll earn us some good money with his stud fees*, Calvin thought.

Two days later, the Marlows loaded their wagon, hitched up the team, and bid farewell to the few emigrants they'd befriended at the tent compound. Calvin rode ahead on Barney to help the Brewsters move out of their dwelling and into a wagon for their return to Ohio. He noticed the pain in Old Man Brewster's back as he tried again and again to throw the harness atop the ill-mannered team. Calvin took the harness from him and threw it up on the small team. "Say hello to Ohio for us," Grace said, "and travel safe." The Brewsters bid them good-bye, clearly happy to be leaving Colorado Territory.

July 1866, Colorado Territory

"So this is our new home, is it?" Grace said with a hint of sarcasm in her faint voice. She looked at the adobe structure as if it were an enemy compound, a space to be conquered. Surveying the one-room cabin, arranging household furnishings in her mind, she finally stared at the dirt floor and said, "Smells to me like a herd of buffalo made a home here for a couple of months. Buffalo tallow, that's what it is! I suspect the Brewsters spread the tallow on the dirt to keep the dust down. Hiram, you take your brother outside and hunt up as much sage as you can find. Hurry now, and don't come back empty-handed. And watch out for those snakes. Plenty of 'em around here."

Calvin helped unload the wagon's contents into their new home and then went to the well to fill the water barrel. He returned to the cabin, where Grace proceeded to bark out orders like an army first sergeant: "Put those pans over there next to the cookstove. We need a sink stand, which you will soon build. The wagon cover needs to be washed in the river, and the dishpan needs a good scrubbing with sand. And, Calvin, see over in the corner, that hole in the roof? You need to cut some sod immediately to cover it. And while you're at it, how about trimming up that scruffy beard of yours?"

Feeling as if he were a lowly private in the army, Calvin went about his chores down at the river with his shotgun, a hatchet, and a file, dragging the canvas bonnet behind. He placed the canvas by the river and looked around for any nearby ducks. His eye caught sight of a lone figure limping down the river road in his direction. As the man came closer, he looked to Calvin to be dressed as an army soldier, carrying a standard army knapsack and wearing the blouse and trousers of an enlisted man but no hat. He carried no weapon, at least none that Calvin could see.

The man stopped on the road to watch Calvin struggle with the canvas in the river and then came toward him. *Yes, an Indian,* Calvin thought, *with that bronze color, those high cheekbones, and the moccasins. The tattoo is that of an Oglala Sioux.* The Indian said not a word as he dropped his knapsack and joined Calvin in the river. He immediately took hold of the opposite end of the canvas to help Calvin submerge it.

He copied Calvin when he gathered up some sand and dead grass from the river's bank and started to scrub the canvas. There was still not a spoken word or attempt to use sign language by either of the two men. After about ten minutes, they both stepped out of the river and spread the canvas on the turf to dry. Calvin smiled at the Indian as a way of saying thanks. The Indian smiled in return, offered his large, muscular hand, and said in a husky voice, "My name Loud Thunder. White man call me "Thunder."

Calvin introduced himself. The Indian responded, "Alvin."

"No. Ca Ca, Ca CAL-vin."

Thunder said, "Calvin" two or three times before he made it clear he wanted something to eat in return for his assistance. Calvin pulled from his pocket two strips of buffalo jerky. He offered one to the Indian, who immediately attacked it. Soon thereafter, Calvin walked up to the cabin and gathered Barney's harness. He started to hitch Barney to the wagon when the Indian sprang up from behind the wagon's side panel, took the reins from Calvin, and gently pulled on Barney to back him up to the wagon's tongue. After he connected the tugs to the tongue, the Indian stood up with a big smile and handed the reins back to Calvin.

Calvin, completely surprised by the Indian's presence and his skill with Barney and the wagon hitch, thanked Thunder with another strip of jerky and then waved good-bye to the Indian as he drove the wagon off to a place Brewster had told him he could find some good sod to cut for bricks.

With his sharpened hatchet, Calvin began chopping into the sod to cut out twenty-four-by-eighteen-inch bricks. He found it to be harder work than he had imagined, made difficult by the thickness of the roots rather than their depth. At the rate he was cutting and with the energy he was expending, Calvin figured the best he could do that afternoon might be to cut six bricks.

As Calvin started chopping out a third brick, he saw the Indian walking toward him. Thunder stood and watched Calvin sweat away at each chop before taking a break to sharpen his hatchet. When Calvin walked over to his wagon to fetch his water canteen, Thunder slipped over to where Calvin had laid his newly sharpened hatchet next to two sod bricks.

Calvin picked up his shotgun from the wagon's bed and stood his ground, expecting the Indian to make a move toward him. He did move, not toward Calvin, but to the edge of a sod cut, where Thunder began to chop into the sod on his own. He chopped fast and more efficiently than Calvin, who noticed how the Indian cut into the sod with the hatchet blade at a slight angle. He put the shotgun back in the wagon and walked over to the Indian, who had cut a brick in half the time it had taken the white man. Calvin took the hatchet from Thunder, pointed to himself, and then took a whack at the turf with the blade perpendicular to the sod. He then pointed to the Indian and took another chop, but this time the blade was at a slight bias off the perpendicular. Calvin spread his hands out while simultaneously shaking his head with a quizzical look.

The Indian motioned for Calvin to come over to where he was sitting on the turf. Thunder wanted Calvin's attention as he knelt down on his hands and knees. Thunder blew hard on the grass, "like the wind," he said. "When the grass bend in the wind," Thunder continued, "the roots grow at angle away from wind. You cut the sod at the same angle as roots. Much easier." Thunder looked up at Calvin and smiled.

Calvin took the hatchet and cut into the sod's roots, now recognizing that the prevailing western winds explained the bias of the root system. "Yes, much easier," Calvin said as he chopped away.

The two men traded off the hatchet and between them cut eight more bricks before hoisting them into the wagon. In the process, Calvin learned that Thunder spoke fair English, in fact better English than he had heard from any Indian he'd met so far. When it was time to go, Calvin motioned for Thunder to hop in, and they rode off toward the cabin. As they sat side by side, Calvin thought about his passenger. *He's probably served as an Indian scout at some army post and is now off on his own. But what post, and did he leave voluntarily, with the permission of the commanding officer? If the officer gave his permission, he'd more than likely have given Thunder a horse for traveling back to his tribe. But instead, the Indian was limping along without a horse, walking in the opposite direction from Sioux lands. If he was a scout, he probably picked up his English at his army post. Is he seeking a job with me? Can he be trusted? Or maybe he's a Sioux spy, gathering information about the location of white settlements to target them for attack. Certainly, the Sioux have reason for revenge and to retaliate against whites who are moving onto their sacred land. I need to keep a close eye on him and find out what I can from others.*

The two men rode back to the river to fetch the dried canvas and spread it over the bricks. Grace watched as they unloaded everything outside the cabin. She whispered to Calvin, "Who's the Indian?" Calvin then introduced Grace to Thunder: "My new helper," he said smiling at Thunder. She had heard about too many Indian atrocities to be comfortable with the "helper." On entering the cabin, the children stared at the Indian in surprise. They didn't fear his smiling countenance as much as they were confused by his presence. Calvin made the introductions all around as Thunder offered his hand to each of the children, an act that put them more at ease.

Calvin immediately sensed the aroma of sage in the room. In his absence, the boys had stomped and hammered sage berries to force out the little moisture in each plant. They had wiped the moisture across the buffalo tallow on the floor and covered everything with sage leaves. "Smells like a prairie in full bloom," Calvin said.

"We'll have a different flavor in here tomorrow," Grace replied with a smile.

Thunder sat with the Marlows at supper, practicing the pronunciation of "Cornelia" while putting away two pounds of cold antelope meat and a helping of string beans. In his deep voice he said, "Thank you . . . mighty good," to Grace. After the meal, he walked to the door, where he waved good-bye to the family.

That night, Grace and Calvin talked about Thunder. "I think he's wanting to work for us, judging by his help to me today. He's one strong lad, probably in his early twenties or younger. It's always hard to tell with an Indian. Sure, we could use some help, at least until the boys are older, but what do we pay him with? We've no extra money, little food to feed him, and no place to bunk him."

Grace made it known that she didn't come all the way out from Vermont to live with a redskin. "Besides, can we trust him, or any Indian for that matter?" Calvin said that on his next trip to town, he'd check around and see if people knew Thunder.

The next day, Calvin cut the tall grass around the outside of the cabin to guard against snakes, with the plan to burn it after the grass dried in October. The biggest challenge remained: planting and growing corn and wheat, which depended on his ability to successfully plow into the deep sod.

Calvin hitched up the oxen team, adjusted the angle of the plowshare, lined up the plow and team adjacent to the last furrow Brewster had cut, and whipped the oxen. They leaned into their yokes, putting heavy pressure on the leather rigging as they pushed off with their hooves into the sod. Nothing moved as the team slipped on the grass. Again, Calvin adjusted the plow's angle, making it shallower this time, and whipped the oxen once again. The team made another difficult pull but with only a yard or so of progress. He halted the team and inspected the furrow—it was less than four inches deep, with roots poking up.

Calvin knew the furrow needed to be at least five inches deep to properly remove the sod and its root base from the underlying soil. *But maybe,* he thought, *grain might grow in shallower furrows cut into the nutritious soil.*

While Calvin ran his plowing experiments and cut some sod bricks over a period of three days, Grace wrote her brother.

July 13, 1866
Dear Jonathan,

We finally made it to Julesburg. Your letter awaited us on our arrival. It's so wonderful to hear from you, especially all the good news about the family. Your

THE GO-BACKER

boys are so grown-up to be doing all those chores on the farm. That your crop is better than last year is a blessing! Nothing could be worse than last year.

I'm so happy to be off the wagon and no longer walking the trail. I know I couldn't take another week of travel. Our shoes are in tatters, and our soles callused. Calvin had to use a rasp on our feet as if he were trimming the hooves of horses.

This country is not at all what we expected. Grass as far as the eye can see in all directions over what at first appears to be a flat landscape. But when we ride through the short "buffalo grass," it is scarred by small gullies, a few water holes, and buffalo wallows. Almost every day we see wildlife—buffalo, white- and black-tailed deer, elk, coyotes, prairie chickens, prairie dogs, badgers, antelope, skunks, rabbits, wolves, fox, ducks, geese. So also do we see snakes.

The rattlers have been with us since the middle of Nebraska. We lived with them on the trail, in and around our camps, and now here around our new sod-and-adobe cabin just west of Julesburg. Last week on the trail, a snake struck an emigrant's stallion. Within hours the poor thing lay down in a fever and shook himself to death, his testicles swollen to the size of bowling balls. Two emigrant women were also struck. The men were more than happy to have an excuse to break out the "snake medicine," otherwise known as whiskey. That and a tobacco-juice poultice helped draw out the poison and save them.

Our new home, if you can call it that, is more like a hut (or a "soddie") made with adobe bricks composed of a mixture of sand and clay and covered with thick grass sod, what folks here call "prairie marble." I'd sure welcome a wagonload of that real marble from home. At least it wouldn't smell so bad and be dripping bugs and worms. There's no wood around here with which to build, and what is available in Julesburg we can't afford.

The biggest surprise for us was learning that we couldn't file for a homestead until the country is surveyed. That will be next year at the earliest, assuming we're still here. It is still not totally clear to us who owns what land in these parts—the Sioux claim some of it as theirs, given to them by the Great Spirit to care for and pass on to their children. The railroad says they own alternate sections here and there. And then we're told by others that most of the land is owned by a single rancher or the government. If you listen to some of the trappers still working around here, they'll tell you that either France or Spain owns the land. We're still trying to figure it all out . . . who owns what and where. Very confusing.

Another thing Calvin learned very quickly is that the sod is so thick, it's impossible to plow and prepare the ground for grains. Folks around here advise us to raise livestock. I don't want to have anything to do with sheep. Remember what happened to ours in Vermont? If we raise cattle, I know they can die just as easily as sheep.

Julesburg isn't much of a town. It serves as a stop for the stage to and from Denver City and the Pony Express. There are but two main streets that intersect each other with some warehouses, a few shops with limited offerings, and, from what Calvin tells me, a telegraph office in one building, and in another a crowded pool hall/saloon, which serves as headquarters for the local troops from nearby Fort

THE GO-BACKER

Sedgwick (formerly Fort Rankin) and a large collection of ruffians, mostly railroad workers and buffalo hunters. We hear the Union Pacific Railroad line will be completed through town later this month. That's why the town is moving to the other side of the South Platte River, to be adjacent to the rail line. There's not much to move, so it shouldn't take long.

I can't tell you how many lies and how much misinformation we have read in the travel books we carried with us. The Prairie Traveler by Captain Marcy is uninformed about the Colorado Territory and its "lush farmland." He exaggerates the safety of the trail we traveled, saying the army is always present to protect travelers against hostile Indians. Nothing is ever mentioned, of course, about the constant danger of cholera, snakes, and the presence of "white Indians"—those highway robbers looking for an easy heist. The other travel books carried by our trail companions are no more accurate or truthful. All are filled with lies and false reports designed to encourage settlement in the West. The railroads profit, so too do the land speculators, of whom there is a new caravan arriving every week.

I know it will be hard to believe, but a few days ago we hired an Indian. His name is Thunder. He showed up one day on the river and volunteered his help to Calvin on a chore. They've made friends and now Thunder won't leave us. Calvin plans to build a small sod hut for him next to our dwelling. He is wonderful with the children, and especially with the horses. He can drive the wagon, help Calvin cut sod, and fetch buffalo chips for me. He is another mouth to feed, but we skimp by.

The boys are well and a big help to Calvin and me. They've turned into good hunters (jackrabbits and prairie chickens). They've also earned some cash in town from the sale of alfalfa seed they collect on the prairie. Like all of us, they could use more flesh, but they do continue to grow. Hiram is almost my height, Sam is to my shoulder, and Cornelia is up to above my elbow. Hard to keep them all in clothes as fast as they grow.

A few days ago at the saloon in town, Calvin ran into a soldier, Sam Boynton from Vermont, with whom he had served in the war. Instead of using the unreliable US mail carried by the Overland Stage Company, Calvin asked his soldier buddy if he would send a letter by way of the army to our Vermont neighbor, the one who owes us the final payment on our note. In the letter, Calvin instructed the purchaser of our farm to send the payment (in specie, not greenbacks) via the army's mail to Boynton at Fort Sedgwick. We know from others that the army's mail is much safer and more reliable than the Overland Stage. Their stages are frequently attacked by Indians or white thieves when not accompanied by an army escort. We expect the money soon.

Our family is getting ready for winter, which I understand can be very severe here. Calvin is patching every adobe wall where he sees the smallest hint of sunlight. We will resod part of the roof and replace the weak rafters with bigger logs (which is very expensive). It is no easy job cutting the twenty-four-by-eighteen-inch sod bricks with a hatchet, spade, or sod cutter, prying them out of the ground, and then hoisting them up to the roof by rope and laying them on a roof or wall, staggered like bricks, with the sod side down to grip the dirt and roots of the layer beneath.

We've traded for some warm buffalo robes, salted away lots of buffalo meat, and I'm making some warmer clothes for the children and knitting squares for another bedcover.

You asked about the Indians near us. They have caused serious trouble in Julesburg in the past, but the army tells us they ran the Indians off to the north. I wish I could believe them, but I can't. Someone in town told Calvin the Indian attacks were in response to the army's killing of all the buffalo in sight, almost always for their hides, leaving the carcasses for the wolves. The army tells us we new settlers need to kill all the buffalo. That way, they assure us, the Indians will go away. I have my doubts. We heard a report just the other day of an Indian raid upriver where they ran off some horses and cattle from a rancher. I sometimes think the army causes us more trouble than they prevent. They call themselves our guardians, like they were a group of angels, but I've yet to see them sprout wings. They'll guard the rail workers but only some of the mail coaches. Not enough troops, they say. With the army around, it is almost impossible for us to live peacefully side by side with the Indians. If the army didn't have Indians to fight, they'd have nothing to do but sit around and drink and whore. Calvin tells me those two activities take up much of their time.

Given the number of stage robberies we hear about, I do hope you receive my letter.

I must now prepare dinner—fresh prairie chicken with some prairie onions and dried apples from Vermont.

Love to everyone from your homesteading sister and family,
Grace

She had just finished her letter when Calvin stomped in to distract her. "How'd the plowing go today?" Grace asked.

"Not good. The sod is too thick for the team to pull through it. Maybe what we need is a bigger team and a heavier plow. I'm going to check one more time in town to see if anyone has successfully plowed in this country. If not, I may go see that Iliff representative about livestock grazing. If we can work out something, I'll sell the oxen and buy us some cattle and maybe a saddle horse. We could sure use one."

"No sheep, please," Grace said.

Calvin removed the bent share from the plow. As he hitched Barney, Thunder appeared by the wagon. Calvin asked Thunder to join him on the ride into Julesburg. The Indian tried to jump up but missed the step with his bad leg. A second attempt put him next to Calvin on the jockey seat.

On the ride, Calvin asked Thunder about his bad leg.

"Happened when some of my tribe attack Julesburg many moons ago. My horse shot, tripped, and I went to the ground, broke my shoulder and leg, with bone sticking out. Army came next morning to gather dead soldiers. Found me lying next to my dead mother and took me prisoner, back to Fort Sedgwick. Doctor fix leg but not heal right . . . big scar and bend in it."

"Did you stay at Fort Sedgwick?" Calvin asked.

"Yes, made an orderly, like a slave for the officers. They all call me 'Red Nigger,' tell me do this, do that, and do it fast. Once I dropped bottle of whiskey. It broke on ground. The

THE GO-BACKER

colonel mad, go into big, big rage, slapped me. Put in cage for two days, fed nothing. After cage, army put me on wagon wheel . . . hands and feet spread and strapped to wheel. Wagon run around in circles. Then it stop. Colonel come to me and say again, 'Red Nigger.' He whip me bad, many times." When Thunder pulled up his blouse, Calvin could see the nasty pink welts on his broad back.

"I run away last moon, hide in Julesburg, sometimes along the river. Eat from garbage late at night, kill town dogs, steal from farms, trap rabbits, prairie dogs. Always hide. Afraid army capture me again and put back on wheel."

"Why not return to your tribe . . . your father, mother, uncles?"

"Mother dead, sister died as baby, father killed on reservation in Dakota. Army tell me they push my tribe way, way north. I do not know where. A long walk and no food. I think better here. What you think, Calvin?"

"Yes, Thunder, you're better off here, but probably not in Julesburg. Soldiers may recognize you in your uniform. It's best to hide under the canvas in the wagon bed."

They rode on into town. The blacksmith inspected the bent share from the plow. He couldn't believe the share hadn't snapped apart.

"I can straighten her out, Calvin, but you'll be back soon for me to fix it again. Like I said last time, you need a stouter plow and a lot more horsepower."

"Is there anyone around here who has plowed successfully in this turf?"

"Only heard of one man. I understand he owned a team of four Belgians that could pull a brick house across the plains from here to Denver City. But even with that, he broke shares like you'd break sticks. He left the country earlier this year. As far as I can tell, Calvin, this ain't plowin' country. Wish it were. Sure have me more business."

After passing a canteen of cold water to Thunder under the canvas, Calvin rode off on the trail toward Fort Sedgwick, wanting to see for himself the fort that the army confidently believed would provide protection for the settlers and the railroad crews.

The military compound was much larger than Calvin had expected. He hunted up his soldier buddy Boynton, who led Calvin on a short tour of the fort. The buildings were constructed of either adobe or logs. Calvin stared with envy at the large piles of logs and milled lumber, construction materials he couldn't afford. Boynton told him the army moved in four hundred cords of firewood by wagon in preparation for winter each year, in addition to twenty tons of hay at the outrageous cost of thirty-five dollars a ton.

"What a luxury, all that lumber and all those logs," Calvin said.

"If you need some scrap lumber, I'll ask my company sergeant if you can haul some off. He's let some other homesteaders take some." Of course, Calvin became excited by the prospect.

As they walked around the post, Boynton pointed out the adobe barracks with double bunks for the two companies of the Second Cavalry, the two-story log officers' quarters, the teamster's adobe home next to the wheelwright shop, the various quartermaster storage buildings (for vegetables, grain, and beef), and a dilapidated log guardhouse.

Calvin asked about a large whitewashed adobe building at the edge of the fort's grounds. "That's our hospital," replied Boynton. "Got a ward with ten beds and private quarters for the post surgeon. The ward is almost always filled with sick or injured soldiers from here or from up in Wyoming, and sometimes a railroad worker or two. That doc, he's a good one. You ever have an emergency, he's your man. Out there beyond the hospital is the bakery and the prefabricated structure for the Second Cavalry band; they only know three and a half tunes."

Pointing to his left, Boynton continued, "That there small frame building with the cross on top is the chapel, and behind it is the post cemetery with its five new graves. Oh, I forgot to point out the sutler's store, right there behind the commissary barracks. He stocks about everything you need but can't afford."

"You get any free time?" Calvin asked.

"Some. We'll go into town to the saloon, order up some pilgrim whiskey, gamble some, maybe sleep or visit the hog farm. Last Sunday our company commander organized a buffalo shoot for us. My platoon won first prize, a half day off next week. Altogether we killed twelve buffalo, took the hides and hindquarters, and left the rest. Them buffalo are real hard to put down. I know we scared off many more than we killed."

"Have you been engaged in any large attacks from the Indians?" Calvin asked, curious about the area's safety.

"Nothing big. The Sioux rarely fight in large numbers. They are more likely to use five to ten braves to attack a ranch or a wagon train, capture some horses and livestock, and retreat fast. As I understand, it's them young renegades who, more often than not, want to make a reputation for themselves. If they fail to kill someone or steal something, at least they can brag to their elders that they've counted coup."

After a pause, Boynton asked, "How about staying around for supper?"

"No thanks. Need to get back to town to see someone about cattle. By the way, what is pilgrim whiskey?"

"It's a local product, made right here in Julesburg real cheap. A concoction of raw alcohol, red pepper, molasses, and a touch of water. It takes a little gettin' used to, but once you do, it's like mother's milk to us soldiers."

Another pause created an awkward silence. Finally, Boynton filled it. "You in the cattle business?"

"Not yet," Calvin responded, "but I hope to be."

With that, the two men said their good-byes, and Calvin rode off toward the telegraph office to hunt up Mr. Iliff's representative, Mr. Jeffries.

"He's over by the machine waiting for a message back from Omaha. Shouldn't be but a minute," the clerk said, looking up from his messy desk.

Calvin made himself comfortable while he sketched a brand for the cattle he intended to buy. He knew enough to design one with straight lines, which would be easier to read on an animal. He thought of all the variations with an *M*: a slash [/] or a bar [—] before, after, above, or below the letter; a cross [x] either below or above the *M*, or maybe a roof [/\] above or a quarter circle [(] below. He decided to keep it simple: with a bar underneath the letter *M*.

Jeffries, an older man with graying hair and a prominent paunch, who appeared irritated with the telegraph message he'd finished reading, walked over to Calvin. Thin lips marked the man's pale face, his glasses were perched dangerously on the tip of his nose, and a loose maroon tie secured the soiled collar of his white dress shirt. Without offering his hand, he announced, "Name's Jeffries. What's it you want?"

"I'm Calvin Marlow, sir. I'm settled out west of town on a quarter section, waiting for the surveyors so I can file on a homestead. One of your cowboys said Mr. Iliff ran cattle around here and said it might be possible for me to run my cattle with his. He suggested I talk with you, sir."

"Where you settled, and what cattle do you have?"

"I just took over the Brewster place three miles west of town, right on the river. Don't own cattle yet, but plan on buying some. What would you advise?"

THE GO-BACKER

"If you're not fenced, and I'm guessing you're not, and you give our cattle access to the river without any hassle, you can run ten yearlings or eight cows with ours."

"Only ten?"

"See here, Marlow, it's a take-it-or-leave-it offer, nothing more and nothing less. Run cattle without my permission or without an approved brand, and you can bet they'll have our brand on them the next day. You'd be surprised what brands our cowboys can fashion with a cinch ring. If you run cattle with us carrying an approved brand, your cattle will be looked after and the heifers or cows bred by our bulls. No deal if you fence your land. Understand?"

"I guess I'll take it. Ten yearlings?"

"That's the deal," Jeffries said as he stared at Calvin without expression. He then asked, "You got yourself a mark or brand?"

"It's an *M* with a bar underneath."

Jeffries looked through a slim notebook. "That'll work. When will you be puttin' 'em in?"

"As soon as I buy the cattle. Know any for sale around here?"

Jeffries said Iliff Cattle Company had some for sale. "Yearlings at five dollars a head. There are about thirty in a pen outside—steers, bullocks, and heifers—all mavericks or slicks with no brands. Our cowboys just collected 'em and brought 'em in here a couple of days ago. Haven't had time to brand 'em. They're in good flesh, and I suspect the heifers are bred to our Shorthorn bulls. If you want, go over there and pick out ten, brand 'em on the left hip, trail 'em home on the south side of the river, and turn 'em out."

"I'll be back tomorrow with some help to cut out the ten and pay you," Calvin replied.

"That'll work," Jeffries said as he offered his hand to Calvin. "One more thing. We don't take greenbacks, just cash."

Calvin walked out of the telegraph office and over to the nearby corral to give the "mavericks" a close look. They were in good flesh, he could tell, and far better than he had expected.

The next day, recognizing that he had no more use for the oxen, Calvin and Thunder walked them with their rigging into town with Hiram mounted on Barney beside them. At the stables, the owner gave a curious look at the Indian as if he recognized him and then inspected the oxen. He offered a fair price, but lowballed Calvin on the price for the harnesses. "A bit worn, they are," the owner commented. Calvin pointed out the strong, thick leather, saying to the stable owner that he wouldn't find another set like them anywhere in or around Julesburg.

They finally settled up on the harnesses before Calvin inquired about a saddle horse.

"Got me here four good ones. Two of 'em just came in earlier this week. Real nice. Brought in by a Sioux who said he worked for the army as a scout. Them horses look to me like mustangs. Indians like to trap 'em, train 'em, bring 'em into town, and sell 'em. By the way, who dis Injun by your side?"

"My helper, works for me."

"Looks to me like he's in the army."

"Not anymore," Calvin declared, hoping to end the interrogation.

Calvin inspected the most muscular of the four geldings, checked his legs, feet, and teeth, and then gave a glance over to Thunder, who shook his head and whispered, "Head too high." Calvin checked another gelding, went through the same inspection procedure, and then threw a saddle blanket at the bay. The horse stood its ground with only a slight flinch at the flying object. Calvin, with a boost from Thunder, climbed on the horse's bare back, rode him Indian style with only a blanket and no saddle and a thin rope in and around the horse's jaw, and put him through various paces, including a gallop out beyond the stable.

"He moves nice, but he's a little goosey, and he sure doesn't have all the speed in the world," Calvin commented to the owner before asking the price for the horse.

"I need forty in gold or I'll trade you straight across for your Morgan." Calvin shook his head and spit on the ground.

Then he said, "The Morgan's not for sale, and I'll bet you didn't give that Sioux half that much."

The owner responded, "Mister, I'll grant you this ain't no racehorse, but he's a sound gelding with some piss and vinegar in him. He's fairly well trained, in good flesh, and safe for anyone to ride, plus I'll throw a hackamore of your choice into the deal."

Calvin looked at the horse once again and then at the owner.

"Those Indians who brought you these horses, they sell only to you or to other horse traders around here too?" Calvin asked as a way to indicate he was willing to look elsewhere for a better deal.

"The only other ones are two old Sioux traders in town. The Indians off the plains will go to them when I won't give 'em their price. Them old men will come out here from time to time with some nice ponies for me. Good traders they are . . . friendly, speak good English. Both ride big, ugly, jug-headed Appys. You can't miss 'em."

"Yes, I know them," Calvin replied. "I've traded with them in town. You have any Indian ponies for sale?"

"Not now. Sold my last one almost a month ago."

"Now about this here gelding, I'll offer you thirty in gold including the hackamore."

The owner thought for a moment before he put his hand out for a shake.

With Calvin riding his new mustang and Thunder driving the wagon with Hiram, they headed to the blacksmith shop for a beaver tail branding iron.

Once mounted, Calvin could tell the new Indian horse was short on manners. He had a nice gait to him but couldn't be reined to change direction or stop. Calvin said to Hiram, "He's a bit nervous and with something of a bad attitude."

Thunder spoke up, "He be better with some training."

At the blacksmith shop, the owner asked, "What you need with a beaver tail?"

"I'll be buying me some yearlings, which I'll need to brand. Can you loan me a beaver tail for a day?"

"Sure can, but what's the brand? Maybe I can make you an iron."

Calvin described the brand and then commented, "I'm only branding ten; it's not worth a new iron for so few."

"Nice brand. No curves in it. Good luck," the blacksmith said as he handed over the beaver tail.

Hiram, Thunder, and Calvin rode back to the Iliff corral, where Calvin once again inspected the yearlings. He selected six steers and four heifers with the biggest frames and the most Shorthorn coloring. An Iliff cowboy helped Hiram and Thunder start a fire for the branding iron before the cowboy rode into the pen, roped the yearlings one at a time, and dragged them to the fire. Calvin, with Thunder's help, branded each yearling on its left hip. Hiram watched intently while he held his nose to block out the bitter smell of burned hair. The cowboy also roped Calvin's new horse, and Thunder tripped him and threw him to the ground. Calvin proceeded to burn his brand on the left hip, just below the "US" brand, which he'd modified with the beaver tail to read "o8."

During a water break, Hiram commented to Iliff's hired man how much he admired the cowboy life, riding the plains and looking after the cattle.

The cowboy was quick to respond. "There ain't much money in cowboyin', I can tell you that. Mr. Iliff, he don't pay all that good: ten dollars a month and a horse. Last winter I thought I'd have to eat the horse, this one I'm riding today. He's a gentle gelding . . . we've been together now a comin' on two years. Only way most of us survive is to trap wild horses. The Indians do the same, break 'em to ride and sell 'em off to a rancher or the stable here in town. Puts some money in our pockets. Hell, us cowboys know that when God turns shit into gold, we'll be born without assholes."

"Sounds about right to me," Calvin responded as he handed the cowboy a quarter and headed off alone to Jeffries's office to pay for the cattle.

Hiram, Thunder, and Calvin trailed the yearlings along the river road back home to where they let them water and rest. Once at home, Hiram ran excitedly up the lane to the adobe structure and shouted to his mother, "Come, Mama, look at our new cattle herd and a new horse."

Grace ran to the river and yelled to Calvin, "Nice-looking critters. So which one do we eat tomorrow for supper?" Her strong voice scattered the yearlings as they ran off to join the larger Iliff herd on the north side of the river.

Calvin was both pleased with and proud of his new herd, even though they'd acted a bit flighty on the road back from Julesburg. *That was to be expected,* he thought, *hadn't seen too many horseback riders in their lives. Couldn't have trailed them without Thunder's help. I must build him a hut next to ours where he can make a home. He deserves something better than the dugout he sleeps in down by the river.*

Calvin had hoped the heifers had been bred over the summer and would be ready to calve in the spring. But with winter coming on, he worried about the snows covering their feed.

Calvin, again with his Indian helper, spent three days cutting a wagonload of turf bricks for Thunder's new soddie.

For the next two weeks, everyone worked together as a hay crew. The older men took turns on the hand scythe, Grace and Cornelia bundling the grass after it had dried and the boys loading the bundles into the wagon pulled by Barney. They stacked the hay against a cabin wall and covered it with a remnant of the wagon's canvas bonnet.

Hoping that Boynton had received Calvin's mailed payment from Vermont, Calvin rode the wagon alone out to the military post, where he found Boynton at the stables, unsaddling his sweat-stained horse.

"Got your package yesterday," Boynton announced excitedly. "Sure as hell is heavy for such a small thing. Must have some specie in there?"

"I sure as hell hope so." Calvin helped Boynton rub down his stout gelding and then checked the horse's legs for sandburs.

"I got it safe under my mattress in my barracks," Boynton assured him.

As they rode through the post, they encountered a cavalry company riding in from a field training exercise. A handsome pair of Belgian workhorses pulled an artillery caisson behind a column of dusty troops.

Calvin inspected the team with a close eye. *They're straight-backed, beautifully muscled, with good legs and hard feet,* he thought, and then commented to Boynton, "Think the army would trade those Belgians for my Morgan stud?"

"Sure," Boynton replied with a smile, "about as likely as Billy Boy promoting me tomorrow to general." Boynton thought for a few seconds and then looked serious. "I did talk to my company sergeant about some lumber for you. He said you could take what you needed from the scrap pile over at the mill. Some good stuff there. I checked it out. Let's go to the barracks first and then to the mill."

"Neatest barracks I've ever seen," Calvin said as the two walked down the aisle of the long adobe building. Thirty blanketed beds, all neatly arranged, faced the center aisle. A large potbellied stove squatted in the middle aisle like a Buddha. "Nothing like the shithole we lived in during our training in Vermont," Calvin said, looking around the barracks.

Boynton pulled a small package from beneath his hay mattress. Calvin noticed immediately that it had been opened.

"You take anything out of here?" Calvin asked.

"No, just checked to see if it was what you were expecting."

"Gold, I hope, and no paper."

"Gold it is, but I didn't count it."

Calvin removed the small canvas pouch from the box, gave it a quick inspection, and held it up in front of Boynton. "Here's the rest of the money from my Vermont farm."

Together they rode over to the mill, where two sawyers worked over a large hardwood log. They cut bolts fourteen inches long that were carried off to two other soldiers who split the bolts into shingles. Other workers produced large floor planks and finished lumber. A Negro private kept the work area cleared of scraps and discarded logs. When asked why the scrap pile was so large, Boynton explained, "It will probably be used for firewood, but with the four hundred cords we received, we got plenty to burn 'til spring."

Boynton helped Calvin load his wagon with mounds of wood scrap, broken shingles, four logs too slim for bolts, and two usable planks. They also grabbed fistfuls of sawdust and packed it into two burlap bags. Calvin thought that what he took from the scrap heap was the biggest and best gift he'd received since leaving Vermont. For all his assistance, Calvin handed Boynton a dollar coin and told his Vermont buddy to buy himself some pilgrim whiskey in town. With the wagon loaded, Barney strained against the weight, but with the encouragement of a whip, the horse picked up the pace and headed home.

Calvin had already given some thought to how he might use the contents of the wagon. The most useful items were the four long logs, two to be used as support posts in Thunder's soddie and the remaining two as replacements for the current posts in the Marlow cabin, which barely buttressed the ridgepoles and the heavy sod roof. The shingles he'd have liked to use on the roof, but there was no lumber upon which to fasten them. They'd serve as good firewood or as shims for the support posts. The two planks he'd fashion into a cabin door, hinged with leather strips at the top of the doorframe to allow it to swing back and forth, and protected on the outside by a large buffalo hide. The luxury of a sawdust floor he knew would appeal to Grace, and when mixed with clay, it would serve as grout to fill cracks and holes in the adobe walls to prevent cold air from leaking into the cabin.

Thunder helped Calvin unload and unhitch the wagon, remove Barney's harness, and take the horse on a short walk to cool him down.

Winter 1866–67, Colorado Territory

The first snows arrived in mid-November with a light wind and enough moisture to keep the pastures open and soften the dry grass for the livestock. But starting in December and continuing into early March, the bitter winds, accompanied by sleet and heavy snows out of the northwest, never let up. Hail made the sound of bullets as it hit hard against the cabin's adobe walls. The snow, with flakes the size of butterflies, fell in no particular pattern, except when blown into five-foot drifts against the cabin walls. Trips to town became virtually impossible and outside chores painful, always with the threat of frostbite. The postmaster told Calvin that Julesburg recorded two weeks of sub-zero weather in January, causing long delays in the mails. When the temperatures froze the South Platte River, all wagon traffic stopped, and across the river no Indians hunted. The buffalo moved in slow motion through the deep snow as their breath formed tiny clouds over their curly black heads, their beards dragging through the drifts.

Days inside the cabin passed slowly. Grace could read from her small collection of books only so many times before boredom overtook the children. She'd create games in which Hiram always took the honors. Calvin repaired harnesses and attended to holes in the roof, more easily managed with Thunder's help as he stood on a bench and moved sod bricks with a shovel handle. Meals consisted of much the same ingredients every day, the only variety being their temperature. Most of all, they missed fresh fruit, vegetables, and milk.

One Saturday, during the cold spell, Calvin ventured into town to purchase whatever food was available—something other than buffalo, longhorn, rabbit, or antelope—and maybe catch up on some local news.

He located two cans of apricots (not his favorite), a can of green beans, a small bag of white beans, a half sack of flour, and, much to his surprise, a jug of fresh milk. He carried the sacks into the saloon to keep the groceries warm while he had a drink. As usual, thirsty soldiers crowded the bar, but no rail workers were present; they had returned to Omaha for the winter. To the delight of the soldiers, the railroad had left behind one sleeping car, a seasonal loan to the military, which quickly converted it into a warm, comfortable home for a madam and three fallen doves willing to nest in Julesburg for the winter. At the bar, Calvin asked one of the soldiers about Boynton.

"Sick he is, in the hospital with half the regiment. Most of 'em with influenza or severe diarrhea. Five already dead, and a good number with the clap. Nothing much movin' out at the post, 'cept for the doc and his assistants. Between the dead, the sick, and the deserters, we're at about 60 percent of our authorized strength."

Calvin had himself another whiskey while in conversation with a sergeant, who reported, "Too cold to be out training or on recon. No reports of Indians; they're probably freezing their balls off like the rest of us. One hell of a winter . . . coldest in ten years is what I hear. We got troops dyin' and desertin'. We'll be diggin' a lot of new graves this spring. I can't believe I volunteered for a five-year stint and all this misery for thirteen greenbacks a month. And after my laundry and the company entertainment fees are deducted, and after the mandatory dollar savings contribution, here I am with nine worthless dollars to spend. Our civilian contractors, like carpenters, bricklayers, and blacksmiths, make at least twice my monthly wage. I know that some deserters from my platoon took their horses, weapons, and saddles with them and sold 'em off in town. They'll fetch far more than what the army pays me for a year's service. And to think that folks are willing to pay good money for an army saddle. That piece of McClellan shit only proves that God produces fools as often as He creates soldiers. If you ask me, you're a dumb coot if you don't desert.

"I heard the army planned to send in some more troops to replace the deserters and the dead, but cancelled their orders because of the sickness at the post. I figure you can die at any army post, warm or cold. Look at what we lost in Virginia's heat during the war. I'm out of this uniform in two months, assuming I don't freeze to death in the meantime. The only good news now is we have buffalo coats. In town, I've been offered some good money for mine, but I'd never sell it. Hell, I wear it all the time, even in bed."

Back at the adobe cabin, Grace finished a letter to her brother.

March 20, 1867
Dear Jonathan,

I did receive your letter written just before Christmas. Thank you for all the family news. You mentioned you had mailed a Christmas present. I never received it. I hope you received mine.

I am sorry to hear of Amos's broken arm. I trust it has healed and he is back to helping you. I hope there are no other illnesses like what we have out here at the nearby army post, Fort Sedgwick. They've had a horrible outbreak of influenza that they can't seem to control. There are many corpses in the storehouse, waiting to be buried after the ground thaws.

I can't remember when I last wrote you, probably last fall. We've had a tough time of it. No way to farm this country, except maybe with a four-horse gangplow, but even then you take a chance of breaking shares in the deep sod. We've bought some cattle locally, and we'll wait until spring to see how they do over the winter.

Our biggest worry is how to survive the cold and snow. We can keep our adobe-sod home warm, but it is always in need of one repair or another. If it is not the sod roof, it is a crack in the adobe wall. Wood—finished lumber, logs, or even tree limbs—is scarce for fires or for building the simplest structure. A day doesn't pass when we don't think about wood, food, and the weather. Forget the Indians. Haven't seen hide nor hair of them since the snows started in late November. See, we built a small "soddie" adjacent to us for Thunder, our Indian hired man. He works for us in return for room and board. It's not much, but he seems satisfied. A small group of Indians raided two farms upriver from us in early December, but when the buffalo moved south, the red devils moved with them.

With some lumber obtained from the army post plus some sod bricks, Calvin has managed to build a small lean-to on the back end of a small corral and close to our water well. We hope it will protect our four heifers against the incessant winds and blowing snow. It took nearly two weeks and the tracking skills of Thunder, plus help from two local cowboys, to find and gather up our four heifers... they're wilder than coyotes. Hopefully, they will stay in the makeshift corral, strengthened with a few flimsy posts, some old telegraph lines (pulled down by the Indians), loads of sagebrush, and sod. The heifers are better behaved now that Cornelia has started to hand-feed them grain and hay. The steers we let fend for themselves on the plains with neighboring cattle.

This country is almost dead in winter. I've seen only a few rabbits, constantly hunted by wolf packs, and some heavy-coated coyotes. Of course, the geese and ducks are gone with the river frozen. The only moving creatures are those bugs, centipedes, spiders, worms, and an occasional snake that drip down from our sod roof, or the mice sneaking in under the front door. I'd have thought they'd freeze to death like most living creatures out here.

You ask if we need anything. We're well fixed for meat, dried fruit (especially Vermont apples), and canned or dried vegetables. I make fresh bread once a week. A fresh egg is hard to come upon, and so also is milk and anything fresh. As you can imagine, if you sent any of those items, they'd never make it to Colorado. In fact, the mails hardly make it this far west, especially in the winter snow and even in the warmer months, when the redskins get on the warpath and start robbing the stages. Most of the "white Indian" robbers make their headquarters in Julesburg, where they spend their "earnings" at the saloon, gambling, drinking, or enriching the prostitutes . . . sometimes all three simultaneously, or so Calvin tells me. The worst enemies to the white Indians are the red ones; they compete for the same object—the gold and silver carried on the poorly protected mail coaches. Both groups would love to *get their hands on the government's paymaster's stage. But it is, as you can imagine, the most heavily guarded wagon in the territory.*

I can barely see out our one window with the snow drifted almost to the roof. Nearly every day Calvin must shovel to keep the window and two small portholes clear to allow light into our cabin. Everything outside has the appearance of white softness, but once outside, we learn quickly it's nature's lure to blue ice and frostbite. I am constantly knitting mittens, mufflers, scarves, and sweaters for the children. You should see how silly Hiram looks in his dirty buckskin trousers, rabbit-skin hat (his Christmas present) pulled down over his ears, bulky buffalo coat, and bright-red scarf wrapped around his neck. I don't think there's an animal on this earth that wouldn't turn in fright and run from him.

Yes, there is something you could send on to me. I could use a bundle of knitting wool (any color), a dozen brass buttons (an excellent trade item with the Indians), and a few new books to read to the children. They have about memorized those that I've read to them over and over again.

Don't worry about us. With God's help, we'll get through this winter one way or another. This place is a test of character, fortitude, and ingenuity, if nothing else.

How I do miss that fireplace in our Vermont farmhouse, the fruit and pine trees, and seeing you, Carrie, and the children. Do take care. We all send warm hugs and love to everyone.

Your prairie sister,
Grace

"I have you some fresh milk and a bag of beans," Calvin announced with excitement as he and Thunder walked through the plank door and stomped the snow off their boots.

Grace disregarded Calvin's proud shopping news, instead pointing over her shoulder. She said angrily, "Look at the roof over in the corner. There's an opening to the North Pole as large as a frying pan. I've tried with the children to move some sod to cover it, but those pieces are all frozen together. I can't move 'em, not a one."

Calvin could see everyone's breath in the cabin. He quickly moved the table to the corner, stepped up on it with his ax in hand, and moved some sod pieces to cover the hole. "Sam, throw a couple more chips in that stove," he called down to his younger son.

Grace inspected Calvin's haul back from town. "Good-looking beans," she commented, "but the flour looks a bit moldy."

"Best I could find, and I was lucky to find any at all."

By mid-March, warm winds had opened some grazing ground. Calvin rode north across the river to check on his steers. He couldn't find a one, but he did encounter an Iliff cowboy who reported that more cattle had survived the winter than expected. Calvin asked about his steers and described the brand. The cowboy, wearing sheepskin chaps and bundled in an army greatcoat, pulled from his pocket a well-worn list, scribbled in pencil. He looked through it and said, "Looks like you lost a steer east of here, Mr. Marlow. Sorry about that. Ken Sodowsky found it dead on February third. No reason noted . . . probably froze to death like most of dem dead ones. You'll get to see your other steers in May or early June, when we move 'em this way."

"I appreciate the news," Calvin replied. "It's gettin' to feel a bit warmer."

"Sure is, and a good thing too." The two men smiled, bid each other a good calving season, and then rode off in different directions.

When he returned home, Calvin stopped at the corral to see how Cornelia was getting along with the heifers.

"Good of you to muck the place clean and water them. They're lookin' heavy with calf," he noted.

"Father, when do you think they'll do it?"

"I'd say they're a couple of weeks off. But we'll need to keep a close eye on them. With the hay about gone, give 'em a bit more grain." Cornelia nodded and then remembered something her father had said back in January.

"Will we need to help the cows calve?"

"May have to with one or two of them. You never know."

"But back in Vermont," Cornelia responded with a frown, "I saw cows just lie down in a pasture and have their calves without help. Are these cows different?"

Calvin didn't want to get into a physiological discussion, so he kept it simple. "These are younger cows having their very first calf."

"I'll sure keep a close watch on them."

"Good girl," Calvin said as he gave her a hug.

About the time the Platte Road's frozen tracks turned to mud, the traffic picked up. Freight wagons made their way west toward Denver City while discouraged miners passed them going east, or, as one wagon sign proclaimed, HEADED HOME.

Calvin talked with one wagon master and his family. The man referred to himself as a "go-backer," the derogatory term for a failed homesteader used by those pioneers who decided to settle and remain in the West. The wagon driver's face reflected a hard if not desperate life: deep furrows cut into his forehead like scars and others sliced through his cheeks before disappearing into his salt-and-pepper whiskers. The wagon stopped

THE GO-BACKER

for water at the river, close to the Marlow cabin. Calvin asked him where he and his family were headed.

"Headed back to Pennsylvania from Latham, now called Greeley, we are," the man replied in a slight Irish brogue, his mouth empty of teeth except for the four yellowed ones in the front.

"Bad luck in Greeley?" Calvin inquired, hoping to gather some information about the territory to the west.

"Aye. This western experiment everyone's so excited about, it's not for us, mate. Couldn't get credit to replace broken equipment or to buy a bigger team, and what little grain we grew in last year's dry summer, a hailstorm ruined most of it. What little of that was left them grasshoppers, clouds of 'em, finished off in three days. Hell, they got themselves so fleshy, they could barely fly: they just hopped around from one plant to the next. 'Tis no country for puttin' a plow in the ground. Bustin' sod is bustin' your health, and the winters . . . look at this arm, mate."

The wagon driver pulled his shirt up to show the stump just below his elbow. "Had it amputated after the frostbite, along with some toes. That's what winter will do to you in this country. No, sir. It's back to the country I know best, western Pennsylvania. And if I had meself a pocketful of sovereigns, I'd move with me family farther back to County Clare, I would."

"You're about the fourth wagon I've seen this week headed back east."

"Well, mate, when God blows us some warmth and dries up this mud, I reckon you'll see more of 'em, you will. I seen a wagon with a handwritten sign on its canvas bonnet said, "A mile to wood, two miles to water, and goin' back to Iowa to stay for good." That's a smart bloke by my way of thinkin.'"

Yelling from the nearby corral interrupted their conversation. "Papa, come quickly, a cow needs help."

"Quiet down, Cornelia. Your yelling only makes the cow nervous. Yes, she is trying to calve. See the calf's feet coming out? Now, while I put a halter on the cow and tie her tight to the corner post, I want you to get the other cows out of the corral. This one doesn't want company. Don't worry, they won't run off. They know where they're fed. Now stop crying while I run to the house and wash my hands."

Within minutes, Calvin returned with a foot-long leather strap with four rawhide loops tied securely to each end. He held the strap in his mouth as he snubbed the heifer closer to the corner post. The animal let out a soft bawl. "Now, Cornelia, I'm going to put a loop around each of the calf's hocks."

"Why are the feet coming first rather than the head?" Cornelia asked.

"That's the way God planned it. Now, no more questions, just pay attention and do what I say."

Cornelia watched closely as Calvin rolled up his right shirtsleeve and reached into the heifer's birth canal with his arm. He pulled his arm out within seconds, recognizing instantly that the calf's head was turned back and not in the proper position to pass through the birth canal.

Calvin explained to Cornelia that he'd have to reach in again and straighten the calf's head to position it properly between its two front legs.

He reached in for the second time and repositioned the calf in preparation for delivery. He removed his slimy arm and whispered, "Success," to a smiling Cornelia. He went to the halter rope to give the cow some slack and then moved quickly to the back of the animal.

"Hand me the strap," he told Cornelia. He placed a loop around each of the calf's hocks, pulled the loops tight, and turned to Cornelia. "Now, this is where I need your help. With this strap, I'll try and pull the calf out. The heifer may want to fall down on her side. Let her do so, but don't be surprised if she tries to get up. When she falls on her side, I want you to sit on her shoulder to prevent her from getting to her feet. She'll probably be moaning or bawling because of the pain as she tries to push the calf out toward me. Now, let's go."

Cornelia moved to the head of the heifer and Calvin started to pull. Just as he predicted, the heifer moaned and fell to her side. Cornelia moved instantly to sit on her shoulder as Calvin continued to pull. He could tell he'd made some progress, but without much help from the heifer, which gave more attention to Cornelia, who kept sliding off its shoulder. Cornelia tried to climb up on the heifer twice more, but the heifer's movement always dislodged her.

"Now, we're going to change positions. You pull on the strap while I sit on the cow," Calvin instructed Cornelia in a reassuring manner. Cornelia moved quickly off the ground to take hold of the strap and started to pull. With Calvin sitting on the heifer, he encouraged Cornelia to keep pulling. Then Cornelia began to cry and said through her tears, "Papa, the calf is going to die."

"No, it isn't," he reassured her. Calvin instructed Cornelia to sit on the ground and brace her feet against the heifer's buttocks to gain some leverage, and then he shouted, "PULL, AND I MEAN HARD!"

Cornelia did as she was told and strained on the strap. All of a sudden, the calf popped out like a cork from a champagne bottle. It wiggled to life on Cornelia's chest as the cow, which Calvin had untied from the post, stood up and instinctively moved to lick her newborn to remove the thin membrane covering it. Calvin pulled Cornelia away from the momma and her calf, blood and slick afterbirth covering Cornelia, while tears of joy flowed down her cheeks. The calf struggled to its feet and, without assistance, found a teat where it sucked hard for the milk, rich in colostrum.

"We have a beautiful calf," Calvin announced with pride. Cornelia cried harder as she reacted to the magic and mystery of birth.

"Now we need to leave the two of them to themselves," Calvin instructed Cornelia. "Everything looks fine, and it is a nice healthy calf. You did a fine job as a midwife. You brought new life into the world." Calvin gave Cornelia a big hug, then father and daughter walked arm in arm up to the cabin.

The Marlow family, including Thunder, wanted to rush down to the lean-to and see the calf. Cornelia told everyone to just peek in and not disturb the mother and her newborn. "They need to be alone so they can get to know each other," Cornelia declared. Her smiling parents nodded in agreement. The two boys only frowned at their now-bossy younger sister.

Early the next morning, under Cornelia's close supervision, the two boys went to the corral to see the newly named Missy. When Hiram reached over to touch the calf, his sister screamed, "*No*, you'll infect it with your filthy hands!" Everyone could tell there'd be no separating Missy the calf and her protector.

Late Spring 1867, Colorado Territory

By mid-May, the snows had melted and the river ran full and muddy. Calvin picketed the new mother cow on a long rope within sight of the cabin to allow her to graze on the fresh grass. Cornelia would move the picket to a new plot every other day. The buffalo returned from their southern feeding grounds and with them came Indian hunters. Soon thereafter, and true to form, the army stirred up the Indians by killing buffalo and letting them rot in the sun.

Calvin rode into town to pick up some turpentine at the hardware store and a set of shoes for the new horse. From there, he rode to Fort Sedgwick where he wanted to check on Boynton's health.

He found his friend resting comfortably at the post hospital.

"The doc says I should be out of here in two days. I've spent too much time here; damned if I didn't come down with diphtheria after I caught the flu. I'm ready for active duty. Can't say I'm in too much of a hurry to get back to my barracks. I've come to like the personal service here, especially the food. The doc pretty much cleared up the influenza around the post. I hear it didn't get itself into Julesburg. Real lucky."

"Glad to know you're on the mend. Any idea what you'll be doing once you're back on a horse?"

"Killing buffalo and chasing Injuns . . . same drill as usual, but probably more dangerous right now. I'm told the Indians are back on the warpath along the South Platte in retaliation for the army's renewed efforts to kill off all buffalo because of the Sioux's refusal to stay on their new reservation. If you were an Injun, how'd you like to be forced to live in the same outdoor pen all your life? They won't stay put, and I guess I can't blame 'em. How're things with you, Marlow?"

"Got ourselves into the cattle business. The cows are almost finished calving. And my five steers are running with Iliff cattle, but I haven't seen hide nor hair of 'em since I bought 'em last fall. For all I know, they could be long gone to Iowa. The Iliff cowboy I see from time to time tells me I should see four of 'em later this month. One of 'em I'll sell the steers this fall. Should have some good weight on 'em by then. I'll keep the cows and calves. You know where we are settled. Next time you ride out that way, stop in for coffee."

Calvin rode off toward home, pleased to know of Boynton's recovery and the army's efforts to limit the influenza outbreak to the post. *They have a good doc out there,* he thought.

As he arrived home, Grace was just finishing a letter to Jonathan.

May 18, 1867
Dear Jonathan,

It has been much too long since I last wrote you, I know. But now that winter is gone (at least according to the calendar), I can attend to correspondence. From February to mid-April, the mails didn't run from here or to here. Either snow, bad roads, or no contractor stopped the mail from time to time. But

THE GO-BACKER

I did receive the package from you with the new books, knitting wool, and brass buttons. They're so much appreciated!

I can safely say we survived our first winter. Not an easy time. We spent most of our waking hours trying to stay warm, which meant patching and repatching our hut. In late February, a heavy snowstorm collapsed the roof close to our cookstove. It took Calvin all day to repair it while we sat in subzero weather urging him to hurry. We repeated the patching process two more times through the winter.

It took forever for spring to arrive. When it did appear, it popped out like a tulip. The wind had finally worn out the snow, leaving behind little rivulets of running water and dun-colored patches of dead grass. The grass crackled underfoot until last week, when warm days brought sprigs of green. Some buffalo are back with the new grass, and they are beginning to shed their winter coats like the rest of us.

Just as it warmed up, poor little Sam came down with a bad fever from an infected tooth. After Calvin pulled the tooth, his fever disappeared, but it has left him weak and in no mood to see another set of pliers.

We sold our team for a lovely saddle horse that we can all ride without fear of injury, We recently had cow calve prematurely, and with the help of Calvin and Cornelia, the calf survived. Our little girl has taken the calf into her care and is proud as a peacock for helping Calvin bring the baby to life. The boys occupy themselves playing down by the river, now that the ice has gone, and gathering dead sage and buffalo chips for the cookstove. I can't get them to stop catching snakes.

I'm not certain this cattle business will support us. We're still living off the sale of our Vermont farm and won't have any new monies until fall, when we sell the five steers (one died this winter). We'll manage. We always have, though I must admit I'm depressed when I see eastbound wagons filled with discouraged homesteaders. One wagon that stopped near us on the river for rest and water was driven by a distraught middle-aged woman accompanied by her three children. She said she and her family had come west last summer to escape the cold winds off Lake Erie in northern New York; now she was headed back east to escape her cruel husband, who, she said, "can freeze to death for all I care." Another family headed east said they were pushed off their small farm near Greeley by a combination of grasshoppers and bankers. We see a few grasshoppers, but nothing like the clouds of them that are reported west of here. As for bankers, not a one around here. The only credit is from the real estate men or a pawnshop. Both are outrageously expensive, charging anywhere from 15 to 30 percent interest a year.

We believe the Indian threat along the river is over. This we've learned from two older Sioux braves with whom we have become trading friends. They mostly trade horses, but this last year we've traded items with them we either brought with us or bought in town—coffee, sugar, tobacco, corn seed, buttons, a needle, and a small kitchen knife—in return for buffalo robes, venison, deerskin clothing, and a wild pony. We couldn't get the Indian out of the pony, so Calvin sold him in town for a good price. Because the braves so much enjoy being around Cornelia, they made her a gift of beaded moccasins... they're beautiful. She won't take them off and even wears them to bed. I wear a long buckskin dress of my own making. If it weren't for our Indian traders, we'd be walking around naked.

An Indian family passed by us not long ago, which reminded me how easy my life out here is compared to that of an Indian squaw. I've seen some with ugly scars on their faces and arms. I understand these scars are self-inflicted after the death of a related warrior. The squaws are used like beasts of burden, carrying heavy loads on their backs or, like dogs, pulling a travois. All the while, the "warriors" ride comfortably on their ponies, usually pulling another travois. The Indians are always moving around, trying to distance themselves from the army or from the overland emigrants, and always in search of buffalo. They see us all as an occupying army.

More people are moving in every day with more and more livestock. Also, we hear of a couple of new stores in town from our closest neighbors, the Carneys. They're from Michigan and, like us, had hoped to raise grain but instead are now trying to raise sheep. They have run into some problems with the cowboys, who threaten to shoot their woolies if they don't move them someplace else. Their young son plays with Sam and Hiram. The Carneys have offered to pay the boys a quarter for each coyote they kill. Hiram brags and tells me he plans to make a hundred dollars this summer.

There are plenty out there to kill. We hear them every evening, along with the wolves, yelling, *serenading, and calling to each other. Sometimes bellowing buffalo, cackling crows, and crickets join them. It's like a chorus, but without a musical conductor or any harmony.*

No more news from the singing prairie. Write soon. I promise to be a better correspondent.

With love,
Grace

The following day, after Calvin hitched Barney to the wagon with the intention of heading into town to mail Grace's letter and to shop for items on her wish list, a line of mounted cavalry soldiers rode up the road toward him. They halted to allow him to pass their ranks. Calvin asked their platoon sergeant, "Does Corporal Boynton happen to be with you boys this morning?"

"No, sir, he's in a different platoon back at the post," the man answered in the distinct deep-Southern accent of a cracker.

"Where you headed, Denver City?"

"I wish. No, we're headed upriver to Pawnee Creek. We have orders to kill all buffalo north of the creek and west of the North Platte, all the way to Julesburg. It's a good bit of territory, but I'm certain we'll have it done in three or four days. Sir, you seen any buffalo around here?" Thunder sat silent and stiff as a board beside Calvin.

"Sergeant, I need to remind you that every time you and your troops go out on a buffalo kill, the Indians blame it on settlers like us and attack us in retaliation for your actions."

"Sir, with Fort Sedgwick just down the road, the Injuns would be foolhardy to attack settlers."

Calvin stared hard at the sergeant and replied, trying to withhold his anger but not his sarcasm, "I haven't heard that you and your soldiers prevented attacks on settlements along

THE GO-BACKER

the river in the past. If I'm not mistaken, the Indians attacked Julesburg twice in the past couple of years and made off with guns, ammunition, flour, sugar, coffee, and liquor, plus half your horses; they also destroyed the stage station and the telegraph lines. Then they ran you soldiers out of the fort. Oh, what great protection you've given us here, Sergeant! How could we expect anything different when over half your troops are galvanized Yankees? When they were Confederates, we kicked their fucking asses in the war, and now the Indians are kicking their asses out here."

The sergeant responded, "Sir, we may be galvanized Yankees, as you say, but let me remind you that after the attack on Julesburg, we ran those redskins up into Wyoming and the Dakota Territories. Congress only recently authorized more troops for the West. I hear we're getting an entire cavalry regiment at the fort, and we've already received a couple of new cannons and some breech-loading rifles. We've also strengthened our fortifications. The savages got nothing to counter our new rifles, and they know it. Generals Sherman and Sheridan want this area wiped clean of Indians. Sherman told our commander he didn't care if they were treaty or non-treaty Indians, just get rid of them. If we kill their buffalo, they'll hightail it back up north or farther west or starve to death."

Pointing his finger at the sergeant and spitting his words out like bullets, Calvin countered, "Listen here, Sergeant, you tell that post commander of yours to tell Sherman and Sheridan back in their comfortable headquarters that they're putting our lives at risk. Yes, we trade with the Indians, and sometimes they give us robes as gifts. We leave them alone and they leave us alone. Then one of your smart-ass generals decides that he wants to starve the Indians to make them peaceful. If you want peace, then leave the buffalo alone. The Indians are hungry and want to hold on to their hunting grounds. But when they defend themselves and their buffalo and you kill them, you report back to your commanders that you're only defending the railroad crews and all those settlers coming out here along the rail lines. That's humbug, and you know it. You know that when you harass the Indians, stir up trouble, and get them to go on the warpath, then you have the excuse to kill them and, in return, receive a promotion. Remember, Sergeant, that when you stir up trouble, we—the settlers—are held to task for your insane actions. JUST LEAVE THE INDIANS ALONE, and everyone will be the better for it."

"Well, sir, I have my orders," the sergeant said to Calvin as he waved his mounted troops forward.

"You dumb ass," Calvin shouted.

"I can have you arrested," the sergeant shouted back over his shoulder.

"For what? Telling you the truth?" The encounter ended as Calvin rode off, thinking of the possible trouble ahead.

He hoped to contact his two friendly Sioux traders so he could warn them of the army's plans and maybe insulate the Marlow family from any Indian retaliation. Calvin hadn't seen the traders in weeks, but he knew they hung out in Julesburg on Saturdays.

Midday Saturday, he headed to Julesburg with Barney and the wagon. In town, he looked around for the Sioux traders but couldn't find them or their horses. He walked by a new general store housed in a ragged former army squad tent. A dirty guard dog lay outside, baring its yellow teeth and scratching fleas on its belly. Calvin gave the dog some space and walked into the store. "Not much inventory," the owner admitted, "but we have a freighter due in here later today with some fancy cotton cloth, canned goods, a few fresh eggs, and maybe even some milk. Name is Daly, just like the sign outside says."

"I'm Calvin Marlow from out west of here. I wish I could wait around for that freighter, but I must get back home." Then, pointing to the few cans on the shelf, he said, "I'll take those

THE GO-BACKER

two cans of peas, plus a half pound of coffee and a fresh lamb rib, if you got it."

"I do, sir."

As Calvin counted out his money, he said to Daly, "Sure hope you make it here. We need your store."

"Much appreciate your business, Mr. Marlow. Come back soon."

Calvin had time to stop at the post office before he made a quick trip to the saloon. He joined a few soldiers at the bar, where he ordered a whiskey. As a way of opening a conversation with a soldier, Calvin said, "Seen some of your troopers out by my farm two days ago, on their way west to kill some buffalo."

"Liked to have gone with them buffalo hunters and get away from the damned fatigue detail at the fort. Besides, that buffalo meat is sure tastier than the tough shoe leather supplied by Iliff," the soldier replied after spitting a wad of tobacco juice in the direction of the brass spittoon. Before continuing, he offered Calvin a chew.

"Nothing I like better than killing buffalos. I knows just where to hit 'em, right behind the shoulder in da lung. It takes 'em a while to go down, but down they'll go in fifty yards. Last time out, just three of us, we run into some Lakota. Would have given them a good chase 'cept the nag I rode didn't move faster than a lame turtle. About the only way to get my gelding to move, like most of our army mounts, is to stick a giant corncob dipped in kerosene up his fucking ass. Trouble was, I weren't carryin' no corncobs that day. You wouldn't wish one of our horses on your mother-in-law. My horse took an arrow in the neck. I couldn't believe what I saw when I pulled that willow stick out. Yes, by God, a metal arrowhead. Ain't never seen one of dem before. My company commander says one or two of the Lakota bands, probably them Brulé, now use 'em if they can trade for the metal from barrel hoops and cans."

Calvin expressed surprise, and to calm the soldier, he changed the subject and asked him about the new officers assigned to the fort.

"Most of 'em are shavetails, just out of West Point. They knows how to read, but can they fight? Do they knows anythin' about the redskins' fightin' tactics, like their sudden raids followed by rapid retreats into desolate country? Another thing about these dumb-ass lieutenants: damned if they don't know French and some Latin and German. Why in hell weren't they schooled in Sioux? We've never run into any Latin-speaking Indians. Good thing too. Our Indian interpreters don't speak Latin or German. And I don't trust a one of them bastards either. These new officers ain't ever seen an Injun before, 'cept maybe in front of a cigar store or on a postal card. Also, they only know how to ride the best-mannered horses on the post . . . and that's about five. Give 'em a green gelding, and they'd sure as hell kill themselves."

"Same old army I served in," Calvin responded before he asked about Boynton.

"His whole company got transferred out to the Seventh Cavalry. I feel sorry for those poor fellows, having to serve under that Custer bastard. I hear he's a real hard-ass and will court-martial you for life if you whip a stubborn mule too hard."

Calvin was about to settle with the bartender when he heard a familiar child's voice. He turned to see his son Sam at the door. "Father, Father, come quickly," Sam said between sobs. "The Indians ran off our cows, and Cornelia is hurt real bad. Hiram and Thunder are helping mother care for Cornelia." He ran over to Calvin and grabbed his shirt to pull his father off the bar stool. Both Sam and Calvin ran out the door, Calvin to the wagon and Sam to the saddle horse. Together they galloped home. As they rode toward the cabin, Calvin could see that the corral had been broken through on the river side, that the horse hoofprints indicated a multiple-horse attack, and that all the cows were gone.

Riding up to the cabin, he saw a thin trail of blood where someone had carried something, maybe an animal, up the hill, past the well, and into the cabin. Inside, Calvin immediately saw Cornelia, her face contorted by pain, stretched out on the table with an arrow deep inside her thigh. Blood streamed from the wound.

"Where have you been?" Grace demanded. "The Indians attacked the corral, where Cornelia was feeding her calf. All of a sudden, they sprang. Thunder and I could hear their war whoops from here, five of them, all mounted with spears, bows, and arrows. But before Thunder could do anything, one of them roped a pregnant heifer and another grabbed the calf. Thunder saw Cornelia chase after her calf. The Indian turned and shot an arrow at Cornelia. I ran to the corral, and with Thunder we carried her up here to the cabin. I tried to pull the arrow from her leg but couldn't extract it. Thunder tried, but when Cornelia screamed in more pain, he stopped."

Calvin looked down at Cornelia, her face distorted by pain. She was breathing hard. "Papa, please stop the pain," Cornelia pleaded through her tears, "and please, I need some water."

Calvin propped up Cornelia's head while Grace slowly administered a half cup of water to her. Calvin then had her swallow a teaspoon of laudanum to help dull the pain. He inspected the arrow and then eased Cornelia onto her side, where he'd have a better angle and more leverage to extract the arrow. Calvin took hold of the peeled-willow shaft and pulled gently at first. Cornelia screamed, but no progress. Calvin brought a chair over to the table, sat, and placed his feet up against the table's edge. Thinking the arrow's barb had caught on the thighbone, he twisted the arrow and pulled hard, as if he were pulling a calf from a cow. Cornelia let out the scream of a soldier whose leg had been blown off by a mortar shell. Finally, the arrow emerged.

Blood poured from the wound, surging with every heartbeat. Thunder helped Calvin apply a tourniquet above the wound and close to the hip. The blood flow slowed. Calvin turned to everyone gathered around Cornelia and, like an army sergeant, began to bark out orders.

"Hiram, gather up the bedding and put it in the wagon. Sam, you help him and give Barney some oats. Grace, fetch me the brandy bottle. Hiram, you and I are taking your sister to see the doc at the fort. Now move it, and I mean like greased lightning."

The boys scattered like mice and had the bedding in the wagon before Calvin, with Thunder's help, gently moved Cornelia to the straw mattress.

"Thunder, I want you to stay here with Grace and Sam in the event those braves return." The Indian nodded in recognition of his responsibility.

Barney trotted from the cabin down to the Platte Road before Calvin put the horse into a lope for the three-mile trip to Fort Sedgwick. He kept looking back at Hiram, who had Cornelia's head in his lap. "How you doing, my dear?" he asked Cornelia.

"I can't stand the pain," she replied in a weakening voice. "Papa, please do something."

Calvin stopped the wagon to give Barney a breather. He pulled from his pocket a small brandy bottle and poured less than a thimbleful into a cup with another spoonful of laudanum.

"This will help with the pain. Just sip it slowly," Calvin said to Cornelia. She sipped the bitter medicine, then dropped the cup and vomited onto Hiram's trousers.

Before Calvin had Barney moving again, Cornelia lost consciousness, and all color drained from her face. Calvin urged the horse to move quickly. By the time they stopped at the fort's front gate, Barney's withers were wet and foam dripped from his mouth. Calvin shouted, "We need to go to the hospital NOW! The guard looked in the wagon, saw the bloody mattress and the unconscious passenger, and rushed to the gate. At a gallop, Barney raced down the fort's main thoroughfare.

Calvin ordered Hiram, "Tie Barney and water him." He lifted Cornelia carefully from the wagon and carried her into the hospital ward. There, he laid her limp body on an empty bed and ran to the end of the ward in search of the doctor.

"Doc, she took an arrow in the thigh. I pulled it out, but I couldn't stop the bleeding. Please see what you can do; she's lost a lot of blood in the last hour." The two men rushed to Cornelia's cot. The doctor inspected Cornelia's pale face as she lay motionless on the white pillow; her milky eyes stared upward, unfocused.

The doctor took her limp hand and held her wrist, then dropped the hand and reached for the side of her throat. He shook his head and looked directly at Calvin. "Sir, I feel no pulse. She has left us."

Calvin sat stunned, tears flowing. He reached for Hiram and pulled him to his chest. No one spoke a word, knowing that anything they said could not comfort the living or revive the dead. The doctor pulled the bloodstained sheet over Cornelia's head and left father and son to grieve alone in the ward's lonely silence.

"Go attend to Barney while I talk to the doc," Calvin gently urged his son. "I'll be back in a minute."

Calvin walked down the ward's aisle. Two soldiers paid their condolences.

"She died from blood loss. I could tell almost immediately by the color of her skin that she had fallen into the deep sleep of death," the doctor said before Calvin asked the question. "There was nothing either of us could have done to save her.

The arrow cut into the femoral artery, and, if not attended to immediately, a wound like that is almost always fatal. I'm sorry for you and your family. You must be a homesteader, correct? Unfortunately, the army does not allow non-military personnel to be buried here at the post."

"I understand. I will take her home with me, and I thank you for your concern and assistance, sir."

The doctor asked Calvin how Cornelia had been injured. He explained with all the details he'd received from Grace and Thunder. "When I pulled the arrow from her leg, I noticed a metal arrowhead. Do you know who uses metal arrowheads?"

"Probably a Sioux band . . . Spotted Tail's Brulé. The post commander tells me they refuse to return to their reservation and will not vacate their traditional hunting grounds along the Platte. Spotted Tail refuses to cooperate with our government about the land and the new wave of homesteaders. I realize you homesteaders are involuntary participants in this conflict."

"That's the God's truth," Calvin replied.

Calvin placed Cornelia gently in the wagon on the clean mattress the doctor had provided. After pulling the sheet over her pale face, father and son headed home.

The two remained silent as they rode beside each other. Hiram kept glancing back at the wagon bed to see if the rough road had shifted Cornelia's body. Calvin stared straight ahead, holding the reins loosely and giving Barney his head. His thoughts were focused on Cornelia and how she always brought joy and laughter at supper, pulling her parents away from the thoughts of their marginal lives.

Did I make the wound worse by twisting the metal-tipped arrow before pulling it out? Maybe I should have pushed it through her thigh, or made the tourniquet tighter . . . would that have stopped the bleeding? Should I have left the arrow in her thigh and let the doc cut it out? Had I not gone to town, could I have scared off the Indians? Have we treated the Indians so badly that they felt compelled to attack our corral and livestock? Was Thunder in any way responsible for the attack? Why couldn't he have stopped it or at least tried to? There must have been something I could have done to save her.

When the cabin came into view, Calvin's thoughts turned to Grace and how to present the horrible news.

Grace, watching from the door, rushed to them as they headed toward the cabin, with Thunder trailing behind. She looked quickly into the wagon's bed and saw Cornelia's auburn hair spread out from under the white sheet that covered her body. Grace pulled back the sheet. She let out a scream as she looked down at the gray face of her dead daughter.

Calvin stepped from the wagon and came to her side. "The doc couldn't save her. She had lost too much blood." Grace ignored Calvin as she struggled to pick up Cornelia from the mattress. Everyone watched Grace as she peeled the bloody sheet from Cornelia's wound. It sounded like someone tearing a piece of paper in half. She removed Cornelia's worn-out Indian moccasins for a keepsake. The sour smell of dead skin remained with them.

With Calvin, Hiram, Sam, and Thunder following behind, Grace carried Cornelia to the cabin's bed, laid her out as if she were a sick patient, placed a pillow under her head, pulled the blanket to her shoulders, and said to Thunder, "Now let's allow her some comfortable sleep."

Tears did the talking through the brief evening meal. "Time for bed," Grace said. Sam changed into his nightshirt, looking confused about his sister's health. The boy had witnessed death on many occasions, back in Vermont and on the trail. He'd never seen anything or anyone come back from death. To Sam, Cornelia looked dead. *Maybe it's different with humans,* he thought. He asked his mother, "Will Cornelia be all right?"

Grace responded immediately, "She'll be fine as soon as she wakes up."

That night Grace inched herself into the bed next to Cornelia, careful not to wake her. Calvin made himself comfortable on the floor next to Grace, with Sam and Hiram beside him. With her left arm, Grace held Cornelia close to her breast, smoothing her hair, kissing her forehead, and whispering love sonnets and prayers to her sleeping daughter. She rearranged Cornelia's legs, noting how stiff they had become. She peeled off the bandage she had applied to the thigh wound, washed it, and put on a clean dressing. "There, that must feel better," she said to Cornelia as she wiped her brow with a cold washcloth and waited patiently for her daughter to awake.

At daybreak, Calvin witnessed Grace gently slide her arm from underneath Cornelia's head, get up, and fetch a glass of water. "She's thirsty," Grace explained. She returned to the bed and pulled Cornelia's stiff jaw open, fabricated a funnel from a piece of paper, and began to slowly drip the water between the girl's teeth until her mouth and gullet filled. A milky fluid overflowed onto Cornelia's chin. Grace wiped her mouth dry and smoothed her hair, and then snuggled close to her daughter once again.

Later that morning, Calvin noticed the anticipation on Grace's face, without any hint of sadness. *This must end*, Calvin thought. He sat on the edge of the bed, took Grace's hand, and spoke softly. "Grace, Cornelia is dead. Don't you understand? God has taken her away and carried her off to heaven. She is safe now."

Grace turned her head abruptly from the pillow and fired back at him, "If you'd showed her any love, she'd come back to us now." Calvin leaned down to give Grace a kiss on the forehead. His display of genuine affection was returned with a spiteful look and a quick slap to the face.

Calvin needed a breath of fresh air as a relief from the smell of death. To occupy himself, he walked up behind the cabin with a shovel to dig the grave. He thought of Cornelia's young beauty, so physically attractive like her mother, with the same blue eyes and auburn hair and an intelligence to understand and accept the unpredictability of life. *Maybe a good life is nothing more than the absence of evil,* Calvin thought. *If I didn't have the rest of my family to feed, I'd put my pistol in my mouth.*

To take his mind off the final act of burial, he walked to the corral and tried in vain to make repairs but gave up in anger. He retrieved an old piece of canvas he had used as a windbreak for the heifers. To further occupy himself, he led Barney to the river, where he washed the canvas and the horse and trimmed Barney's burred mane. Soon Grace walked slowly down the path in his direction.

Her eyes red and her posture slouched, Grace said in a weak yet firm voice, "Cornelia will not be buried here near these savages. We will take her away with us."

Has she finally accepted death? Calvin asked himself, but he needed clarification from Grace. "Away to where?" he asked.

"Back home to Vermont."

"Back to that rock pile? Remember why we left Vermont, Grace?"

"Yes. I remember all your grand ideas about the bright new life we'd have out here on free land among the peaceful Indians with the army's protection. I've had my fill of it, Calvin. I'm tired of taking responsibility for our children. Now one child is dead, thanks in part to you."

"And what is that supposed to mean?"

"Had you been here rather than off at the bar in town with all your drinking buddies, Cornelia would be sitting here with us, alive and as beautiful as ever."

"Grace, I don't know how we could have prevented the Indian raid. You know, as do others along the river, that the Indians want revenge against all who threaten their lives, like the army and the new settlers, including ourselves."

"Then we should never have come here," Grace shot back.

"In hindsight, maybe so. There were so many things we didn't know about this country when we moved here."

"You convinced me, Calvin, that you had done ample research—read newspapers, guidebooks, magazines, farm journals, even talked with the army in Burlington."

"Well, I was convinced and, I thought, on good authority, like the agricultural magazines and Mr. Greeley's paper. I read too many boosters and believed their exaggerations, if not lies. They didn't do us any favors. But remember the positive reports we heard on the trail coming out here?"

"Yes, all lies," Grace spit out. "I need to get out of here, and I'm not leaving Cornelia behind."

"Maybe we can give this country another try. It looks to me as if our cattle venture will be profitable." Calvin hoped his lie might brighten Grace's spirits.

"To hell with another try and your stupid cattle venture. I've tried as long as I can to make this home, but not anymore. We need to go back to our real home and take Cornelia with us."

"Home to Vermont? That's what we escaped from," Calvin reminded Grace as he nodded toward the east.

"And from one prison to another. I want OUT OF HERE . . . the only companion I have here is the wind, and the children when they're not frozen in bed. Are you afraid to go back? Afraid to be thought of as a quitter, some sort of worthless, no-account failure, a damned go-backer, a weakling, not man enough to face the challenges of the frontier? You're more concerned about your personal reputation, Calvin, than the welfare of your family."

Grace then turned her criticism away from Calvin to homesteading. "You know as well as I that every settler out here lives in a constant state of anxiety. What new test will God devise for us tomorrow? Yes, we know how to live in snow, but not in the winds that produce nine-foot drifts. And what about those winter days when the temperature drops forty degrees in three hours? Yes, we've lived through droughts, but not ones that last nine months. We've faced enemies before, but nothing like the Indians, who burn homes and scalp their white enemy."

Calvin tried to calm Grace. "We've worked hard here to make a home for ourselves and the children. We have food on the table and own some livestock. Things will get better, I know it."

"And will we have to give up another child or ourselves to the savages before things get better?"

"The army is sending more troops to Fort Sedgwick for our increased protection."

"You and your goddamned army—that's all I hear. How perfect the army is, how they will protect us. Don't you understand, all they do is tell lies about how great and safe this country is, that more troops are coming here, isn't that wonderful? All that means is more soldiers at the bar and more prostitutes to serve them. No, it won't work out for us, Calvin. As long as the army's policy is the systematic annihilation of the Indian, I don't want to be near anyone in uniform. We need to leave and take Cornelia with us. I want her to be buried in a proper graveyard, undisturbed, and guarded over by our Christian God. If I have to, I'll take Cornelia back in a cart, with or without you."

Calvin gave some thought as to how to transport Grace back east. If he had ice readily available he could keep Grace from decomposing. Or, as he remembered from his Civil War days, he could use arsenic to embalm the body. With neither ice nor arsenic available, he accepted the fact he'd be transporting a decomposing Grace back to Vermont.

Calvin spent the rest of the day building a coffin from the spare lumber he'd taken from the fort's salvage pile. He hinged the top plank of the coffin with leather strips, knowing that Grace would want to view Cornelia from time to time on the trip east. In the afternoon, he rode the wagon into town with Hiram and Thunder, purposely leaving Sam and all his questions at home with Grace. In the wagon, they carted two empty barrels, three extra buffalo robes Calvin had obtained from the old Sioux traders, plus the bent plow. At Mr. Jeffries's office, he sold back to the Iliff Cattle Company all his steers in addition to the two soddies and the homestead claim, for a total of sixty dollars in specie. With the proceeds, he purchased some supplies—a new canvas bonnet and oak tongue for the wagon, a bag of threepenny nails, a small bucket of grease, rifle and shotgun ammunition, matches, gunpowder, and two finished boards for a new wagon seat. At the grocery store, he filled one barrel with corn and the other with bags of flour, salt, dried beans, dried vegetables, and fruit. He completed the order with cans of baking powder, a small bag of sugar, and some tobacco plugs for trade with the Indians. At the livery stable, he inspected eight oxen, all recently purchased from the Sioux, who'd bought them from overland homesteaders the previous fall. After the Indians fattened the animals on summer grass, they put the oxen up for resale before winter at a healthy profit. Calvin selected two stout, equally sized oxen, paid up, tied them to the wagon, and headed for the blacksmith shop. There he offered the plow for sale but refused the counteroffer. He did have a tire and a small metal sleeve on the running gear replaced. When he offered to settle up, the blacksmith responded, "Forget the bill, Calvin. Sure sorry to hear about your daughter. From what I see passing through town, you'll have some company headed back east. You take care of yourself and your family on your way back."

The next morning, Calvin wrapped Cornelia in the piece of clean canvas and placed her on a bed of straw in the casket. On the back end of the wagon, he built a platform with braces to carry the casket on their journey east.

Together the family and Thunder packed the farm wagon, carefully placing the new canvas bonnet over the willow bows, arranging barrels, crates, the stove, and the clothes chest, and leaving enough floor space for two mattresses.

Calvin explained to Thunder as best he could why the family wanted to return east to their original home, and that he could not join them on their trip. "We've no room in the wagon and little food." To make the trip less inviting to Thunder, Calvin added, "We will, I know, run into army troops on the trail. They may still be on the lookout for you."

Thunder nodded his understanding but then asked, "What about Cornelia?"

"She'll go with us, and we'll bury her after we cross the Missouri River, many days from here, east toward the rising sun," Calvin responded and then continued, "I have a gift for you."

Calvin pulled from his pocket a twenty-dollar gold piece and handed it to Thunder. The Indian took the coin, and to show his appreciation, he crossed his arm over his heart.

"Wait," Thunder said as he went to his hut and returned with a three-colored horsehair bridle. "For you, Calvin, my friend," he said and then crossed both his arms over his chest, a signal of lasting friendship.

The family loaded onto the wagon as Calvin filled the water barrel at the well, and with their new oxen team, they headed down the South Platte toward Nebraska and points east. No one showed much emotion except for the boys, who waved to Thunder, who was standing by his hut, waving back.

Calvin purposely did not push the oxen; they, like everyone else, had to reaccustom themselves to trail life. But as the oxen learned to work together—to pull even and come to know verbal commands—Calvin picked up the pace, wanting to make better time than they had on the trip west. The prevailing western winds helped push the wagon east, in addition to the boys' increased confidence driving the oxen, either with whips from the wagon seat or walking beside them on the ground.

Come evening, they'd make camp close to other travelers, some headed west with optimism, others headed east with failed dreams. On the third day, Calvin purposely circumvented Fort McPherson, hoping to avoid the post commander, who'd probably ask if he'd ever reported the murder of his train captain on the trail west the previous year. Calvin guided the Marlow wagon north on a three-mile detour around the fort, and under a bright moon, they stopped just short of the same burned area they had encountered a year before. They made camp with another party headed east, the McCanns, a family of four who spoke with the soft accent of the upper South. The two families shared supper together that evening, venison Calvin had shot the day before. At the dishwashing detail adjacent to their wagon, the oldest of the McCann boys asked Hiram, "What's that ridin' on the back of your wagon?"

Without looking at the wagon, he answered, "A casket."

"Got a body in it?"

Hiram was quick to reply, looking directly at the boy as he pulled a plate from the dirty wash water. "It is not a body. It's my sister."

After the meal, Calvin sat alone with Jake McCann, whose ragged clothing and grim countenance suggested he'd seen some hard times somewhere along the line. A holstered pistol rested on his left hip.

"Headed back to North Carolina. Grasshoppers took most of what we growed in that Greeley area," McCann volunteered. "What about you?" he inquired of Calvin.

"We've also had our problems. Goin' back to what was our home in Vermont." Calvin went on to explain Cornelia's death and Grace's depression as the reason for their turnaround.

"We never had no trouble with them redskins, on the trail, or in or out of Greeley. Had more damned trouble with some ornery Yankees in the area." McCann's comment immediately caught Calvin's attention.

"Like what kind of trouble?"

"Look, mister, I don't want to get into any disagreements with you after that fine supper you fixed. But to answer your question, I said some things about General Sherman them folks didn't like. You have to understand that Sherman and his soldiers near the end of the war came to our North Carolina farm outside of Goldsboro on the Neuse River lookin' for food. Must have thought we belonged to the caviar set. They pointed to our two sows, some flour, and the half-filled corncrib. I told 'em we didn't sell to Yankees. On orders from Sherman, or so I was told, them bluecoats immediately shot the sows, took our three sacks of flour, and with the corn loaded everything into their wagon. They took our niggers, then burned our home and barns, but left us our rig. We hid out upriver for almost a year with some kin until the war's end.

"So when folks tell me what a fine soldier General Sherman is, I can smell his dirty ass all the way out here. And the last man who challenged my comments about Sherman now lies buried in a Greeley lot. I nailed him before he even got a hand on his pistol. A group of men calling themselves the Greeley Protection Committee visited me soon after the shooting and strongly suggested I move on down the road. So here I am. Do you collar?"

"Yes, I understand."

Calvin let the conversation die in the event McCann decided he wanted to take on another Yankee, especially one who had served with that badass General Billy.

The next morning the two families broke camp. Calvin kept his distance from the McCanns and made certain to select a midday rest area and evening campsite far behind the North Carolinians.

That night before supper, Calvin checked the coffin to see if it had survived the rough trail. No evident cracks, but it did emit a distinct odor, which everyone knew came from Grace but refused to mention. He unhitched the top and lifted it. The shoulders of Cornelia's bloated body lay bare where the canvas cover had fallen open. Green-headed flies gathered on her upper torso, where they had laid their eggs. Small maggots, looking like little small white worms, crawled from underneath the canvas. When Calvin pulled the canvas back from Cornelia's head, larger maggots appeared, crawling in and out of her mouth, nose, eyes, and ears. The putrid stench of decomposing flesh surrounded him as he slammed down the casket's cover. To close off any access to more flies, he immediately began sealing the coffin with strips of an old cotton shirt dipped in axle grease, especially the small air leaks between the boards on the top and sides of the casket. Finally, he nailed the top of it shut, not to be opened again. Still, the disgusting odor prevailed.

While he worked on the coffin, Grace walked up from behind him and asked what he was doing. The truth would devastate her, Calvin knew. "Nothing much. Just patching a few cracks in Cornelia's casket." But still the smell of decomposed flesh filled the air.

"I want to see her," Grace pleaded as she reached for the coffin's lid.

Calvin grabbed her arm. "No, you don't," he responded in a firm manner, almost as if issuing a military command. She backed off, tears gathering on her sunburned cheeks. That night she cried herself to sleep. *Has she accepted the death of Cornelia?* Calvin wondered. *Will she ever heal?* He wasn't certain.

The next evening, a single man riding a well-muscled bay gelding with a "US" brand on its left hip rode up to the Marlow camp. "Mind if I set up here close to you and the river?" he inquired.

"Plenty of room around here, so make yourself comfortable," Calvin replied. Grace spent suppertime writing a letter to her brother while the boys and Calvin shared a light meal, mostly dried apples. The heavily bearded visitor, his whiskers as thick as a horsehair mattress, dressed in a combination of army clothes and civilian rags, sauntered over to the Marlow fire and offered Calvin a cigar.

"Thanks, I don't smoke. Where you headed?"

"Back home to Upstate New York. And you?"

"Vermont."

"We all have some miles to make."

"That's the truth," Calvin responded and then asked, "Looks to me, judging from your horse, you been with the army?"

"Yup, just ended my enlistment in a cavalry regiment. Nasty duty chasing dem Indians from Montana to Nebraska under the command of an incompetent colonel."

"Seems to be several of them in the army these days," Calvin remarked.

"Sounds like you have firsthand knowledge."

"Served in the war with a volunteer Vermont regiment. Had a superb colonel, however."

"You're lucky. My colonel got us lost once in the Nebraska Sandhills. We had to be rescued by another regiment. Real embarrassing. He didn't know nothin' about fightin' Indians. When we'd run across some redskins, we'd ride up on them, bugles blasting away, all the while movin' in useless and dangerous formations designed by the German army. The redskins hid out behind rocks and sagebrush and picked away at us one at a time. More often than not, we got our ass kicked real bad. By the time we reloaded our Springfields—poured powder, inserted a ball, rammed home the charge, set the primer, cocked the hammer, and fired—a redskin had already fired off three arrows at his target.

"Had enough of the army, I have. I ate better in jail than anything we had on the trail. I'm sure tired of tough horse meat, and the poor pay that goes with it, equipment that breaks down, rank horses that only know how to buck and break your back."

"Looks to me like you're riding a pretty good gelding," Calvin commented.

"Yes, when I took my unauthorized leave from the army I rode away on an army mule. Headed directly for the mines near Denver City, but couldn't cover my daily expenses. Just east of Denver, I traded the mule and my boots to a young Kiowa for this here horse. It appears that the redskin stole it from the army. See the 'US' brand? So as a deserter with a stolen horse, I guess I'm just another outlaw on the trail."

"Yes, there are many outlaws on the trail," Calvin responded without mentioning his own status and his need to avoid the law. "If I were you, I'd sure as hell change that brand before an army patrol sees it."

"Like how?"

"Take that brass buckle from your cinch, heat it up, and use it like a branding iron. Put a tail on the underside of the *U* so that it looks like a *Y*, then burn a slash across the middle of the *S* so that it looks like an *8*, and presto, you got yourself a fancy new brand, Y8."

"Sounds like you've done this yourself?"

"No, but I did learn a thing or two in the army."

As they bid each other a good night's rest, Calvin advised the soldier to stay safe and avoid army patrols. He then returned to his wagon, where Grace had finished her letter to her brother.

> *June 30, 1867*
> *Dear Jonathan,*
>
> *I've received no recent letters from you before we left the Julesburg post office. I assume everything is going well with you and family.*

THE GO-BACKER

We have suffered greatly this early summer due to a horrible tragedy. Out of nowhere, savage Indians attacked us and in the process killed Cornelia. We thought we had made friends with the local Indians by way of two minor but older chiefs with whom we traded back and forth. But the chiefs could not prevent a small group of Sioux braves from attacking us. All the recent trouble started when the army began a wholesale slaughter of buffalo. Small parties of Sioux braves began retaliatory raids against homesteaders like us on the South Platte. At our place, the Indians stole some livestock and in the process killed Cornelia when she tried to protect her young calf.

I cannot leave this country fast enough. Calvin wanted to stay on and try to make a go of it with cattle. I want to return to Vermont, but Calvin isn't so sure. In the end, I wanted to leave more than Calvin wanted to stay.

He says if we go back to Vermont, we'll be "farming rocks" and he'll be reminded of the Civil War, memories he wishes to forget. In any event, we're heading east now, carrying Cornelia with us. There is nothing in Colorado I'll miss. I was so tired of using whatever energy I had just to survive what God sent our way, and it was usually something different each day. The wind, carrying tons of dirt, never let up. Our dinners consisted of dust washed down by alkali water. No wonder my hair is turning gray! If Calvin killed a prairie chicken, we celebrated as if it were Christmas. The children haven't seen a drop of fresh milk in four months, but plenty of moldy bread.

Besides, I never considered that place home. I always felt like an uninvited guest in Colorado. I never considered our shack, cabin, hut, or soddie—whatever one wants to call it—our home. We had hoped to build something bigger and more substantial to protect us better from the incessant winds and snows. A home, as I remember ours in Vermont, must include some personal items—curtains, handmade rugs, or a piece of family furniture to which one is attached by way of memory. Absolutely nothing in our soddie felt like home. Father's portrait, which we brought with us, was smashed by some falling boxes on our way there. I was ready to leave then.

I don't know if I can survive the trip back east. God has struck us a horrible blow. My little girl is now dead from an Indian arrow. When she died from a loss of blood, her face expressed the horrible pain from her wound. Calvin tried to save her, but to no avail. She is no longer with us but back in God's pocket.

If and when we return to Vermont, I hope we will find a small farm where we can profitably grow some grain and maybe raise some livestock. Fortunately, we have some money left over from the sale of Mother's farm (thanks to you), the sale of our Julesburg land and soddie, and the sale of our livestock. Hopefully, we will find a farm, something appropriate that we can afford. Wherever it is we settle, we'll bury Cornelia in a Congregational church graveyard close to our new home.

Don't bother to write, because your letter probably will not catch up with us. We are headed for Omaha, and from there hopefully back to Vermont by way of the same route we took coming out.

THE GO-BACKER

The boys are well, which is amazing given their horrible diet. Like the rest of us, they miss their dear sister.

With love, your sister,
Grace

July 1867, Headed Home

The Marlows made their way once again on the Oregon Trail toward Omaha. There were more wagons headed east than moving west—disillusioned family farmers, like the Marlows, freighters returning for another load of supplies ordered by Denver City hardware stores, wagons piled high with buffalo bones for a fertilizer plant, a heavily armed mail coach, and scores of half-starved miners shuffling along through the dust.

One former California miner who had retraced his path back to the Oregon Trail by way of San Francisco told Calvin at a midday water hole stop that discouraged miners swarmed the California port seeking passage back to the East Coast. "You got to be lucky to find the gold. The only folks I seen who make money in California, especially in San Francisco, are the codfish aristocracy, those who came out here with money already in their pockets, like some of them Boston merchants. Most miners I knew agreed with whoever said, 'The best way to make money is to inherit it.' I didn't inherit nothin'. That's why I'm headed back to New Bedford, lookin' to take up my previous work on a whaler. I seen what must be almost a hundred whaling ships from back home now anchored in the mud of San Francisco's harbor. Only a few were headed home, and those that were, I couldn't afford. That's why I'm a walkin'. My sister in her letter tells me that four hundred whalers have left Nantucket for the gold mines . . . the island is almost totally vacant. The few whaling companies that survive in Nantucket and New Bedford are now payin' top dollar for experienced crewmen. As best as I can figure it, there's more money spearing whales in the East right now than huntin' gold in the West today or tomorrow."

That same afternoon, the Marlows came upon four Sioux warriors who were holding up a six-wagon train, demanding their usual tribute for passing through their land. One wagon master kept shaking his head at the warrior in charge, who'd dressed himself in an army captain's tunic. As Calvin came up to the train, he shouted to the wagon master, "Mister, you'd be wise to accommodate them unless you're lookin' for an Indian haircut."

Calvin hoped the Indians might let his eastbound wagon pass without demanding a tribute, in return for his assistance with the stubborn wagon master. Unfortunately, the strategy didn't work, he quickly discovered. After a brief negotiation and the payment of two plugs of tobacco, the Marlows proceeded eastward.

The family passed near where Calvin had killed Ferguson the year before. He reminded himself of his good fortune not to have run into the law. He hadn't even been questioned by a single authority since the murder.

They made good time to Omaha, delayed only once by an unseasonably heavy rain and a loose tire. As the trip progressed, the oxen learned to work as a coordinated team, and the boys accustomed themselves to the long hours of boredom, interrupted only by shifts driving the oxen or accompanying Calvin on short hunting outings. He took pride in how

Hiram and Sam had become excellent trappers and handy with a pistol and the shotgun.

In Omaha, the Marlow wagon lined up once again, awaiting space on a ferry to Council Bluffs, Iowa, on the opposite side of the Missouri River.

Grace remarked, "Folks I've met in the lineup with us don't seem as friendly or willing to be neighborly like those we met coming west."

"They're worn out like the rest of us," Calvin responded, glancing at the lineup. "They probably faced some hard times wherever they tried to make a go of it. I suspect those heading west with big smiles and warm greetings look at us as deadbeats or failures, lazy-to-the-bone bummers, and lacking the character to be successful in life. I wonder how many of those smiling faces will be lined up here next year, like us, waiting for the ferry to take them in the opposite direction. Their eyes will have changed from bright beacons of light to deep holes of darkness."

Barges crowded the docks at Omaha with labor gangs, mostly Negroes unloading crates and rails destined for points west. Calvin had to agree with Grace's observation about Omaha when she said, "I haven't seen any evidence this hellhole has changed much in a year. The same number of drunks are staggering around, probably mostly Irish."

But Calvin did come to the Irish's defense: "Now, Grace, don't get all huffy about the Irish. I spent almost two years fighting alongside them, and good soldiers they were."

"Maybe so, but they've sure not brought the civilization that's so desperately needed to the West, nor has your army."

"There you go again, criticizing the army."

"And why not? It is because of them damned fools we lost our daughter."

Fortunately, the opportunity presented itself for Calvin to change the subject and avoid another spat with Grace. He announced, "It looks like we'll load onto the next ferry. Get ready for the trip."

"Give me a minute or two," Grace replied. "I need to clear some space on the wagon floor for Cornelia. I think she'll be safer in here with us than riding that platform on the back end of the wagon. Would you and the boys move Cornelia to the floor?"

Once safely across the river at Council Bluffs, the Marlows off-loaded their wagon and headed for the road they had come out on through Iowa. Calvin preferred to travel alone when possible. That way, he figured, they'd avoid train delays and any diseases other wagons might be carrying, the danger of road bandits notwithstanding. Also, they wouldn't have to explain the presence of a coffin riding on the back of their wagon.

Early August 1867, Iowa

At the crossing on the Iowa side, Calvin entered the ferry office to inquire if they had any news of the weather farther east. An older clerk responded, "Buddy, this ain't no weather station. You want a ticket? If not, make way for them that do." On a board next to the clerk were posted advertisements for Omaha stores and services—hardware, dry goods, wagons, doctors, real estate—and a couple for Council Bluffs. One poster advertised quarter and half sections for sale at two to three dollars an acre, depending upon the location along the Union Pacific Railroad line in and around the central Iowa town of Newton. Those wishing to inspect this land, "with its deep, rich soils," were advised to "take the Union Pacific train from Council Bluffs headed to Des Moines and on through to Newton. There are two trains daily (except for Sunday) to Des Moines and points east: 9:00 a.m. and 2:30 p.m. The stationmaster at Newton will provide the traveler with directions to the nearby sale properties."

Calvin asked Grace to come look at the poster. She said, "I know Iowa is well known for its grains, especially corn, but we have no idea what the land is like around Newton." Calvin agreed, but suggested that maybe they should make some inquiries.

Calvin approached a man waiting in line for a ticket who appeared to be a farmer by his dress, tanned face, and rough hands. "Sir, excuse me. I may be headed to Newton. Can you tell me if it is good country to grow grain?"

"Ain't never been there, but I hear it is good grain country."

"If Iowa is such good country for farming, why are you leaving?" Calvin inquired.

"Just sold my small farm east of here at a nice profit. Thought I'd look for a bigger place farther west and make me an investment. Know of any place?"

"Sir, the only advice I have for you is to stay away from eastern Colorado if you're looking to farm. Farther west may be good, but I can't vouch for it. Good luck to you."

"And the same to you, sir. I 'preciate your advice."

Grace made her own inquiries among the women who looked to be of a farming background.

One woman had no idea where Newton was located. Another woman said she had a sister-in-law near Newton. "They seem to be doing OK, except for a tornado scare earlier this summer. No harm done. However, I know they had a good crop." Another woman, with a heavy German accent, threw more questions back at Grace than she was willing to answer.

"Maybe we should look at it. Nothing is lost except time. Could be good country or a region of sand or mud," Calvin suggested. "We probably passed near it on our way west. I don't remember, but I do recall seeing some beautiful cornfields in Iowa. Probably best if you stay here with the children and the wagon while I take the train to Newton and inspect the land. I'd be away no more than three days. Besides, the cost for all of us to take the train would be expensive."

"So you're suggesting I stay in this town alone with the children? I'd rather live in hell, thank you very much."

"It's not like the town is swarming with Indians," Calvin said in an attempt to mollify Grace.

"Maybe not, but there are plenty of drunk soldiers to take their place," Grace countered. After further discussion, Grace gave in to Calvin's suggestion, but only when Calvin found everyone a comfortable and safe camp with other go-backers.

That evening with the children and Grace camped around a fire, a woman camper screamed, "INDIAN!" when a shadowy figure appeared behind the sparks. Fearing the worst, everyone stared at the shadow to confirm the presence of an Indian. Hiram jumped to his feet, ran to the Indian, threw his arms around him, and said in a loud voice, "It's Thunder!"

September 1867; Newton, Iowa

September 1, 1867
Dear Jonathan,

How I have missed news from home, but as you know we've been on the road since leaving northeast Colorado well over two months ago, and I understand how impossible it was to send us letters.

Since leaving Julesburg and my last letter, we made our way back to the Oregon Trail and retraced our route to Council Bluffs. There we learned of some lands for sale by the Union Pacific. Calvin took a train from Council Bluffs to investigate the advertised land located in Newton, Iowa, in the middle of the state. He liked it and put down a small deposit. A local bank made a decent loan to Calvin to finalize the purchase of 160 acres. So here we are on a quarter section, a half mile from the rail line and three miles from Newton. We're living in the wagon and a small shack on wheels, which Calvin bought from a homesteader. The homesteader told

Calvin the shack had been used two or three times on various homestead claims within the county as proof of an "improvement" to the land office. All the public land has already been claimed around this area of Iowa. That is why Calvin bought from the railroad. It's a small town of about a six-hundred people with all the shops we need, including a medical doctor. Calvin learned from the banker that the Newton area is very productive corn country with frequent rains—certainly an improvement over dry Colorado.

The most amazing thing happened to the children and me while we were camped waiting for Calvin to return from his train trip. Who shows up at our camp but Thunder, our hired man in Colorado. Without us being aware, he followed us on foot from Julesburg all the way to Omaha, where he stole an army horse to help him swim across the Missouri River to Council Bluffs. Thunder told me, "Horse, he good swimmer, better than Thunder." There, he found our camp and presented himself to us. He scared the daylights out of our fellow campers. He's been a great help to Calvin—preparing the land, planting a crop, and building a small cabin.

We've already collected some nice stud fees from Barney, whose conformation and muscle pattern is much appreciated by Iowans. The money we took with us from Colorado—from selling our cattle and the soddie on the quarter section—we put toward the land here and some lumber, at very reasonable prices. We've begun to build us a cabin, which we hope to add to next year.

Finally, and to my delight, we joined the Congregational church, one of three churches in town. Nice, friendly folks and a wonderful minister. We've waited all this time, until we could find a new home and a church, to bury Cornelia. It is here, nearby us, in the church's beautifully shaded graveyard, that we plan to bury Cornelia tomorrow. I will be able to visit her from time to time.

I am so happy to be settled here, though I do miss you and your family. Please be assured that we are in good health and spirits here in Iowa.

With love to all,
Grace

The next day the minister conducted the short service at the burial site. He quoted from Psalm 23 and said at the end, "Cornelia shall dwell in the house of the Lord forever."

Grace watched as the two boys, Calvin, and Thunder lowered the casket into the ground. Calvin and Thunder stood together over the deep hole, and before any soil covered the wooden box, Thunder dropped into the grave a new pair of moccasins and said, "You will need these, Cornelia, on your long journey to a new life."

THE END

ACKOWLEDGMENTS

Many thanks to three writers for their helpful assistance with this book and others: William Adler, Richard Moe, and Steve Horn. They are special friends who never fail to offer creative suggestions and helpful criticisms. Others who have assisted me are Syd Nathans, Faith Marcovecchio, Anne Price, Joan "Cactus" Baker, Pamela Cannalte, and the talented team at Girl Friday Productions, especially Lindsey Alexander, Monique Vescia, Rachel Marek, and Devon Fredericksen. Willie Matthews, my neighbor and Irish whiskey partner, again provided the beautiful front cover. And as always, my wife, Deedee, gave me the opportunity and encouragement to write.

ABOUT THE AUTHOR

Photo © 2017 Karen Onderko

Peter R. Decker is the author of five previous books: *Fortunes and Failures: White-Collar Mobility in Nineteenth-Century San Francisco*; *Old Fences, New Neighbors*; *"The Utes Must Go!": American Expansion and the Removal of a People*; *Saving the West*; and *Red, White & Army Blue*. After receiving his Ph.D. in American history from Columbia University, Decker taught history and public policy at Columbia, Barnard College, and Duke University. He served as an army officer in the U.S. and in Laos, and subsequently served as Colorado commissioner of higher education and Colorado commissioner of agriculture. Decker currently lives with his wife on his cattle ranch in Ridgway, Colorado.

Made in the USA
Columbia, SC
29 October 2017